Henry James

Henry James OM (15 April 1843 – 28 February 1916) was an American-British author regarded as a key transitional figure between literary realism and literary modernism, and is considered by many to be among the greatest novelists in the English language. He was the son of Henry James Sr. and the brother of renowned philosopher and psychologist William James and diarist Alice James.

He is best known for a number of novels dealing with the social and marital interplay between émigré Americans, English people, and continental Europeans. Examples of such novels include The Portrait of a Lady, The Ambassadors, and The Wings of the Dove. His later works were increasingly experimental. In describing the internal states of mind and social dynamics of his characters, James often made use of a style in which ambiguous or contradictory motives and impressions were overlaid or juxtaposed in the discussion of a character's psyche.(Source: Wikipedia)

Literary works:

Watch and Ward (1871)
Roderick Hudson (1875)
The American (1877)
The Europeans (1878)
Confidence (1879)
Washington Square (1880)
The Portrait of a Lady (1881)
The Bostonians (1886)
The Princess Casamassima (1886)
The Reverberator (1888)
The Tragic Muse (1890)
The Other House (1896)
The Spoils of Poynton (1897)
What Maisie Knew (1897)
The Awkward Age (1899)
The Sacred Fount (1901)

THE SELECTED WORKS

OF
HENRY JAMES
VOL. 11 (OF 36)

GEORGINA'S
REASONS

THE PATH OF
DUTY

PAPER SKY CLASSICS

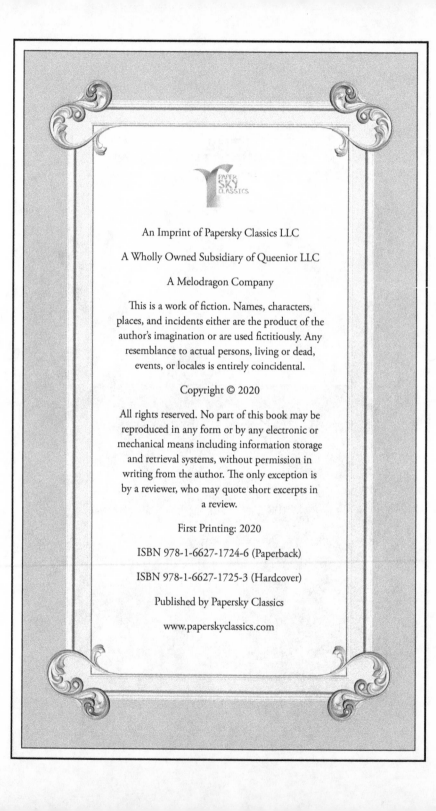

An Imprint of Papersky Classics LLC

A Wholly Owned Subsidiary of Queenior LLC

A Melodragon Company

First Printing: 2020

ISBN 978-1-6627-1724-6 (Paperback)

ISBN 978-1-6627-1725-3 (Hardcover)

Published by Papersky Classics

www.paperskyclassics.com

Contents

THE
SELECTED
WORKS
OF
HENRY JAMES
VOL. 11 (OF 36)

GEORGINA'S REASONS

PART I.

I.

She was certainly a singular girl, and if he felt at the end that he did n't know her nor understand her, it is not surprising that he should have felt it at the beginning. But he felt at the beginning what he did not feel at the end, that her singularity took the form of a charm which—once circumstances had made them so intimate—it was impossible to resist or conjure away. He had a strange impression (it amounted at times to a positive distress, and shot through the sense of pleasure—morally speaking—with the acuteness of a sudden twinge of neuralgia) that it would be better for each of them that they should break off short and never see each other again. In later years he called this feeling a foreboding, and remembered two or three occasions when he had been on the point of expressing it to Georgina. Of course, in fact, he never expressed it; there were plenty of good reasons for that. Happy love is not disposed to assume disagreeable duties, and Raymond Benyon's love was happy, in spite of grave presentiments, in spite of the singularity of his mistress and the insufferable rudeness of her parents. She was a tall, fair girl, with a beautiful cold eye and a smile of which the perfect sweetness, proceeding from the lips, was full of compensation; she had auburn hair of a hue that could be qualified as nothing less than gorgeous, and she seemed to move through life with a stately grace, as she would have walked through an old-fashioned minuet. Gentlemen connected with the navy have the advantage of seeing many types of women; they are able to compare the ladies of New York with those of Valparaiso, and those of Halifax with those of the Cape of Good Hope. Eaymond Benyon had had these advantages, and being very fond of women he had learnt his lesson; he was in a position to appreciate Georgina Gressie's fine points. She looked like a duchess,—I don't mean that in foreign ports Benyon had associated with duchesses,—and she took everything so seriously. That was flattering for the young man, who was only a lieutenant, detailed for duty at the Brooklyn navy-yard, without a penny in the world but his pay, with a set of plain, numerous, seafaring, God-fearing relations in New Hampshire, a considerable appearance of talent, a feverish, disguised ambition, and a slight impediment in his speech.

He was a spare, tough young man, his dark hair was straight and fine, and his face, a trifle pale, was smooth and carefully drawn. He stammered a little, blushing when he did so, at long intervals. I scarcely know how he appeared on shipboard, but on shore, in his civilian's garb, which was of the neatest, he had as little as possible an aroma of winds and waves. He was neither salt nor brown, nor red, nor particularly "hearty." He never twitched up his trousers, nor, so far as one could see, did he, with his modest, attentive manner, carry himself as one accustomed to command. Of course, as a subaltern, he had more to do in the way of obeying. He looked as if he followed some sedentary calling, and was, indeed, supposed to be decidedly intellectual. He was a lamb with women, to whose charms he was, as I have hinted, susceptible; but with men he was different, and, I believe, as much of a wolf as was necessary. He had a manner of adoring the handsome, insolent queen of his affections (I will explain in a moment why I call her insolent); indeed, he looked up to her literally as well as sentimentally; for she was the least bit the taller of the two. He had met her the summer before, on the piazza of a hotel at Fort Hamilton, to which, with a brother officer, in a dusty buggy, he had driven over from Brooklyn to spend a tremendously hot Sunday,—the kind of day when the navy-yard was loathsome; and the acquaintance had been renewed by his calling in Twelfth Street on New-Year's Day,—a considerable time to wait for a pretext, but which proved the impression had not been transitory. The acquaintance ripened, thanks to a zealous cultivation (on his part) of occasions which Providence, it must be confessed, placed at his disposal none too liberally; so that now Georgina took up all his thoughts and a considerable part of his time. He was in love with her, beyond a doubt; but he could not flatter himself that she was in love with him, though she appeared willing (what was so strange) to quarrel with her family about him. He did n't see how she could really care for him,—she seemed marked out by nature for so much greater a fortune; and he used to say to her, "Ah, you don't—there's no use talking, you don't—really care for me at all!" To which she answered, "Really? You are very particular. It seems to me it's real enough if I let you touch one of my fingertips! "That was one of her ways of being insolent Another was simply her manner of looking at him, or at other people (when they spoke to her), with her hard, divine blue eye,—looking quietly, amusedly, with the air of considering (wholly from her own point of view) what they might have said, and then turning her head or her back, while, without taking the trouble to answer them, she broke into a short, liquid, irrelevant laugh. This may seem to contradict what I said just now about her taking the young lieutenant in the navy seriously. What I mean is that she appeared to take him more seriously than she took anything else. She said to him once, "At any rate you have the merit of not being a shop-keeper;" and it was by this epithet she was pleased to designate most of the young men who at that time flourished in the best society of New York. Even if she had rather a free way of expressing general indifference, a young lady is supposed to be serious enough when she consents to marry you. For the rest, as regards a certain haughtiness that might be observed in Geoigina Gressie, my story will probably throw sufficient light upon it She remarked to Benyon once that it was none of his business why she liked him, but that, to please herself, she did n't mind telling him she thought the great Napoleon, before he was celebrated, before he had command of the army of Italy, must have looked something like him; and she sketched in a few words the sort of figure she imagined the incipient Bonaparte to have been,—short, lean, pale, poor, intellectual, and with a tremendous future under his hat Benyon asked himself whether *he* had a tremendous future, and what in the world Geoigina expected of him in the coming years. He was flattered at the comparison, he was ambitious enough not to be frightened at it, and he guessed that she perceived a certain analogy between herself and the Empress Josephine. She would make a very good empress. That was true; Georgina was remarkably imperial. This may not at first seem to make it more clear why she should take into her favor an aspirant who, on the face of the matter, was not original, and whose Corsica was a flat New England seaport; but it afterward became plain that he owed his brief happiness—it was very brief—to her father's opposition; her father's and her mother's, and even her uncles' and her aunts'. In those days, in New York, the different members

15

of a family took an interest in its alliances, and the house of Gressie looked askance at an engagement between the most beautiful of its daughters and a young man who was not in a paying business. Georgina declared that they were meddlesome and vulgar,—she could sacrifice her own people, in that way, without a scruple,—and Benyon's position improved from the moment that Mr. Gressie—ill-advised Mr. Gressie—ordered the girl to have nothing to do with him. Georgina was imperial in this—that she wouldn't put up with an order. When, in the house in Twelfth Street, it began to be talked about that she had better be sent to Europe with some eligible friend, Mrs. Portico, for instance, who was always planning to go, and who wanted as a companion some young mind, fresh from manuals and extracts, to serve as a fountain of history and geography,—when this scheme for getting Georgina out of the way began to be aired, she immediately said to Raymond Benyon, "Oh, yes, I 'll marry you!" She said it in such an off-hand way that, deeply as he desired her, he was almost tempted to answer, "But, my dear, have you really thought about it?"

This little drama went on, in New York, in the ancient days, when Twelfth Street had but lately ceased to be suburban, when the squares had wooden palings, which were not often painted; when there were poplars in important thoroughfares and pigs in the lateral ways; when the theatres were miles distant from Madison Square, and the battered rotunda of Castle Garden echoed with expensive vocal music; when "the park" meant the grass-plats of the city hall, and the Bloomingdale road was an eligible drive; when Hoboken, of a summer afternoon, was a genteel resort, and the handsomest house in town was on the corner of the Fifth Avenue and Fifteenth Street. This will strike the modern reader, I fear, as rather a primitive epoch; but I am not sure that the strength of human passions is in proportion to the elongation of a city. Several of them, at any rate, the most robust and most familiar,—love, ambition, jealousy, resentment, greed,—subsisted in considerable force in the little circle at which we have glanced, where a view by no means favorable was taken of Raymond Benyon's attentions to Miss Gressie. Unanimity was a family trait among these people (Georgina was an exception), especially in regard to the important concerns of life, such as marriages and closing scenes. The Gressies hung together; they were accustomed to do well for themselves and for each other. They did everything well: got themselves born well (they thought it excellent to be born a Gressie), lived well, married well, died well, and managed to be well spoken of afterward. In deference to this last-mentioned habit, I must be careful what I say of them. They took an interest in each other's concerns, an interest that could never be regarded as of a meddlesome nature, inasmuch as they all thought alike about all their affairs, and interference took the happy form of congratulation and encouragement. These affairs were invariably lucky, and, as a general thing, no Gressie had anything to do but feel that another Gressie had been almost as shrewd and decided as he himself would have been. The great exception to that, as I have said, was this case of Georgina, who struck such a false note, a note that startled them all, when she told her father that she should like to unite herself to a young man engaged in the least paying business that any Gressie had ever heard of. Her two sisters had married into the most flourishing firms, and it was not to be thought of that—with twenty cousins growing up around her—she should put down the standard of success. Her mother had told her a fortnight before this that she must request Mr. Benyon to cease coming to the house; for hitherto his suit had been of the most public and resolute character. He had been conveyed up town from the Brooklyn ferry, in the "stage," on certain evenings, had asked for Miss Georgina at the door of the house in Twelfth Street, and had sat with her in the front parlor if her parents happened to occupy the back, or in the back if the family had disposed itself in the front. Georgina, in her way, was a dutiful girl, and she immediately repeated her mother's admonition to Beuyon. He was not surprised, for though he was aware that he had not, as yet, a great knowledge of society, he flattered himself he could tell when—and where—a young man was not wanted. There were houses in Brooklyn where such an animal was much appreciated, and there the signs were quite different They had been discouraging—except on Georgina's pail—from the first of his calling in Twelfth Street Mr. and Mrs. Gressie used to look at each other in silence when he came in, and indulge in strange, perpendicular salutations, without any shaking of hands. People did that at Portsmouth, N.H., when they were glad to see you; but in New York there was more luxuriance, and gesture had a different value. He had never, in Twelfth Street, been asked to "take anything," though the house had a delightful suggestion, a positive aroma, of sideboards,—as if there were mahogany "cellarettes" under every table. The old people, moreover, had repeatedly expressed surprise at the quantity of leisure that officers in the navy seemed to enjoy. The only way in which they had not made themselves offensive was by always remaining in the other room; though at times even this detachment, to which he owed some delightful moments, presented itself to Benyon as a form of disapprobation. Of course, after Mrs. Gressie's message, his visits were practically at an end; he would n't give the girl up, but he would n't be beholden to her father for the opportunity to converse with her. Nothing was left for the tender couple—there was a curious mutual mistrust in their tenderness—but to meet in the squares, or in the topmost streets, or in the sidemost avenues, on the afternoons of spring. It was especially during this phase of their relations that Georgina struck Benyon as imperial Her whole person seemed to exhale a tranquil, happy consciousness of having broken a law. She never told him how she arranged the matter at home, how she found it possible always to keep the appointments (to meet him out of the house) that she so boldly made, in what degree she dissimulated to her parents, and how much, in regard to their continued acquaintance, the old people suspected and accepted. If Mr. and Mrs. Gressie had forbidden him the house, it was not, apparently, because they wished her to walk with him in the Tenth Avenue or to sit at his side under the blossoming lilacs in Stuyvesant Square. He didn't believe that she told lies in Twelfth Street; he thought she was too imperial to lie; and he wondered what she said to her mother when, at the end of nearly a whole afternoon of vague peregrination with her lover, this bridling, bristling matron asked her where she had been. Georgina was capable of simply telling the truth; and yet if she simply told the truth, it was a wonder that she had not been simply packed off to Europe.

Benyon's ignorance of her pretexts is a proof that this rather oddly-mated couple never arrived at perfect intimacy,—in spite of a fact which remains to be related. He thought of this afterwards, and thought how strange it was that he had not felt more at liberty to ask her what she did for him, and how she did it, and how much she suffered for him. She would probably not have admitted that she suffered at all, and she had no wish to pose for a martyr.

Benyon remembered this, as I say, in the after years, when he tried to explain to himself certain things which simply puzzled him; it came back to him with the vision, already faded, of shabby cross-streets, straggling toward rivers, with red sunsets, seen through a haze of dust, at the end; a vista through which the figures of a young man and a girl slowly receded and disappeared,—strolling side by side, with the relaxed pace of desultory talk, but more closely linked as they passed into the distance, linked by its at last appearing safe to them— in the Tenth Avenue—that the young lady should take his arm. They were always approaching that inferior thoroughfare; but he could scarcely have told you, in those days, what else they were approaching. He had nothing in the world but his pay, and he felt that this was rather a "mean" income to offer Miss Gressie. Therefore he did n't put it forward; what he offered, instead, was the expression—crude often, and almost boyishly extravagant— of a delighted admiration of her beauty, the tenderest tones of his voice, the softest assurances of his eye and the most insinuating pressure of her hand at those moments when she consented to place it in his arm. All this was an eloquence which, if necessary, might have been condensed into a single sentence; but those few words were scarcely needful, when it was as plain that he expected—in general—she would marry him, as it was indefinite that he counted upon her for living on a few hundreds a year. If she had been a different girl he might have asked her to wait,—might have talked to her of the coming of better days, of his prospective promotion, of its being wiser, perhaps, that he should leave the navy and look about for a more lucrative career. With Georgina it was difficult to go into such questions; she had no taste whatever for detail. She was delightful as a woman to love, because when a young man is in love he discovers that; but she could not be called helpful, for she never suggested anything. That is, she never had done so till the day she really proposed—for that was the form it took—to become his wife without more delay. "Oh, yes, I will marry you;" these words, which I quoted a little way back, were not so much the answer to something he had said at the moment, as the light conclusion of a report she had just made, for the first time, of her actual situation in her father's house.

"I am afraid I shall have to see less of you," she had begun by saying. "They watch me so much."

"It is very little already," he answered. "What is once or twice a week?"

"That's easy for you to say. You are your own master, but you don't know what I go through."

"Do they make it very bad for you, dearest? Do they make scenes?" Benyon asked.

"No, of course not. Don't you know us enough to know how we behave? No scenes,—that would be a relief. However, I never make them myself, and I never will—that's one comfort for you, for the future, if you want to know. Father and mother keep very quiet, looking at me as if I were one of the lost, with hard, screwing eyes, like gimlets. To me they scarcely say anything, but they talk it all over with each other, and try and decide what is to be done. It's my belief that father has written to the people in Washington—what do you call it! the Department—to have you moved away from Brooklyn,—to have you sent to sea."

"I guess that won't do much good. They want me in Brooklyn, they don't want me at sea."

"Well, they are capable of going to Europe for a year, on purpose to take me," Geoigina said.

"How can they take you, if you won't go? And if you should go, what good would it do, if you were only to find me here when you came back, just the same as you left me?"

"Oh, well!" said Georgina, with her lovely smile, "of course they think that absence would cure me of—cure me of—" And she paused, with a certain natural modesty, not saying exactly of what.

"Cure you of what, darling? Say it, please say it," the young man murmured, drawing her hand surreptitiously into his arm.

"Of my absurd infatuation!"

"And would it, dearest?"

"Yes, very likely. But I don't mean to try. I sha'n't go to Europe,—not when I don't want to. But it's better I should see less of you,—even that I should appear—a little—to give you up."

"A little? What do you call a little?"

Georgina said nothing, for a moment. "Well, that, for instance, you should n't hold my hand quite so tight!" And she disengaged this conscious member from the pressure of his arm.

"What good will that do?" Benyon asked,

"It will make them think it 's all over,—that we have agreed to part."

"And as we have done nothing of the kind, how will that help us?"

They had stopped at the crossing of a street; a heavy dray was lumbering slowly past them. Georgina, as she stood there, turned her face to her lover, and rested her eyes for some moments on his own. At last: "Nothing will help us; I don't think we are very happy," she answered, while her strange, ironical, inconsequent smile played about her beautiful lips.

"I don't understand how you see things. I thought you were going to say you would marry me!" Benyon rejoined, standing there still, though the dray had passed.

"Oh, yes, I will marry you!" And she moved away, across the street. That was the manner in which she had said it, and it was very characteristic of her. When he saw that she really meant it, he wished they were somewhere else,—he hardly knew where the proper place would be,—so that he might take her in his arms. Nevertheless, before they separated that day he had said to her he hoped she remembered they would be very poor, reminding her how great a change she would find it She answered that she should n't mind, and presently she said that if this was all that prevented them the sooner they were married the better. The next time he saw her she was quite of the same opinion; but he found, to his surprise, it was now her conviction that she had better not leave her father's house. The ceremony should take place secretly, of course; but they would wait awhile to let their union be known.

"What good will it do us, then?" Raymond Benyon asked.

Georgina colored. "Well, if you don't know, I can't tell you!"

Then it seemed to him that he did know. Yet, at the same time, he could not see why, once the knot was tied, secrecy should be required. When he asked what special event they were to wait for, and what should give them the signal to appear as man and wife, she answered that her parents would probably forgive her, if they were to discover, not too abruptly, after six months, that she had taken the great step. Benyon supposed that she had ceased to care whether they forgave her or not; but he had already perceived that women are full of inconsistencies. He had believed her capable of marrying him out of bravado, but the pleasure of defiance was absent if the marriage was kept to themselves. Now, too, it appeared that she was not especially anxious to defy,—she was disposed rather to manage, to cultivate opportunities and reap the fruits of a waiting game.

"Leave it to me. Leave it to me. You are only a blundering man," Georgina said. "I shall know much better than you the right moment for saying, 'Well, you may as well make the best of it, because we have already done it!'"

That might very well be, but Benyon did n't quite understand, and he was awkwardly anxious (for a lover) till it came over him afresh that there was one thing at any rate in his favor, which was simply that the loveliest girl he had ever seen was ready to throw herself into his arms. When he said to her, "There is one thing I hate in this plan of yours,—that, for ever so few weeks, so few days, your father should support my wife,"—when he made this homely remark, with a little flush of sincerity in his face, she gave him a specimen of that unanswerable laugh of hers, and declared that it would serve Mr. Gressie right for being so barbarous and so horrid. It was Benyon's view that from the moment she disobeyed her father, she ought to cease to avail herself of his protection; but I am bound to add that he was not particularly surprised at finding this a kind of honor in which her feminine nature was little versed. To make her his wife first—at the earliest moment—whenever she would, and trust to fortune, and the new influence he should have, to give him, as soon thereafter as possible, complete possession of her,—this rather promptly presented itself to the young man as the course most worthy of a person of spirit. He would be only a pedant who would take nothing because he could not get everything at once. They wandered further than usual this afternoon, and the dusk was thick by the time he brought her back to her father's door. It was not his habit to como so near it, but to-day they had so much to talk about that he actually stood with her for ten minutes at the foot of the steps. He was keeping her hand in his, and she let it rest there while she said,—by way of a remark that should sum up all their reasons and reconcile their differences,—

"There's one great thing it will do, you know; it will make me safe."

"Safe from what?"

"From marrying any one else."

"Ah, my girl, if you were to do that—!" Benyon exclaimed; but he did n't mention the other branch of the contingency. Instead of this, he looked up at the blind face of the house—there were only dim lights in two or three windows, and no apparent eyes—and up and down the empty street, vague in the friendly twilight; after which he drew Georgina Gressie to his breast and gave her a long, passionate kiss. Yes, decidedly, he felt, they had better be married. She had run quickly up the steps, and while she stood there, with her hand on the bell, she almost hissed at him, under her breath, "Go away, go away; Amanda's coming!" Amanda was the parlor-maid, and it was in those terms that the Twelfth Street Juliet dismissed her Brooklyn Romeo. As he wandered back into the Fifth Avenue, where the evening air was conscious of a vernal fragrance from the shrubs in the little precinct of the pretty Gothic church ornamenting that charming part of the street, he was too absorbed in the impression of the delightful contact from which the girl had violently released herself to reflect that the great reason she had mentioned a moment before was a reason for their marrying, of course, but not in the least a reason for their not making it public. But, as I said in the opening lines of this chapter, if he did not understand his mistress's motives at the end, he cannot be expected to have understood them at the beginning.

II.

Mrs. Portico, as we know, was always talking about going to Europe; but she had not yet—I mean a year after the incident I have just related—put her hand upon a youthful cicerone. Petticoats, of course, were required; it was necessary that her companion should be of the sex which sinks most naturally upon benches, in galleries and cathredrals, and pauses most frequently upon staircases that ascend to celebrated views. She was a widow, with a good fortune and several sons, all of whom were in Wall Street, and none of them capable of the relaxed pace at which she expected to take her foreign tour. They were all in a state of tension. They went through life standing. She was a short, broad, high-colored woman, with a loud voice, and superabundant black hair, arranged in a way peculiar to herself,—with so many combs and bands that it had the appearance of a national coiffure. There was an impression in New York, about 1845, that the style was Danish; some one had said something about having seen it in Schleswig-Holstein.

Mrs. Portico had a bold, humorous, slightly flamboyant look; people who saw her for the first time received an impression that her late husband had married the daughter of a barkeeper or the proprietress of a menagerie. Her high, hoarse, good-natured voice seemed to connect her in some way with public life; it was not pretty enough to suggest that she might have been an actress. These ideas quickly passed away, however, even if you were not sufficiently initiated to know—as all the Grossies, for instance, knew so well—that her origin, so far from being enveloped in mystery, was almost the sort of thing she might have boasted of. But in spite of the high pitch of her appearance, she didn't boast of anything; she was a genial, easy, comical, irreverent person, with a large charity, a democratic, fraternizing turn of mind, and a contempt for many worldly standards, which she expressed not in the least in general axioms (for she had a mortal horror of philosophy), but in violent ejaculations on particular occasions. She had not a grain of moral timidity, and she fronted a delicate social problem as sturdily as she would have barred the way of a gentleman she might have met in her vestibule with the plate-chest The only thing which prevented her being a bore in orthodox circles was that she was incapable of discussion. She never lost her temper, but she lost her vocabulary, and ended quietly by praying that Heaven would give her an opportunity to *show* what she believed.

She was an old friend of Mr. and Mrs. Gressie, who esteemed her for the antiquity of her lineage and the frequency of her subscriptions, and to whom she rendered the service of making them feel liberal,—like people too sure of their own position to be frightened. She was their indulgence, their dissipation, their point of contact with dangerous heresies; so long as they continued to see her they could not be accused of being narrow-minded,—a matter as to which they were perhaps vaguely conscious of the necessity of taking their precautions. Mrs. Portico never asked herself whether she liked the Gressies; she had no disposition for morbid analysis, she accepted transmitted associations, and she found, somehow, that her acquaintance with these people helped her to relieve herself. She was always making scenes in their drawing-room, scenes half indignant, half jocose, like all her manifestations, to which it must be confessed that they adapted themselves beautifully. They never "met" her in the language of controversy; but always collected to watch her, with smiles and comfortable platitudes, as if they envied her superior richness of temperament She took an interest in Georgina, who seemed to her different from the others, with suggestions about her of being likely not to marry so unrefreshingly as her sisters had done, and of a high, bold standard of duty. Her sisters had married from duty, but Mrs. Portico would rather have chopped off one of her large, plump hands than behave herself so well as that She had, in her daughterless condition, a certain ideal of a girl that should be beautiful and romantic, with lustrous eyes, and a little persecuted, so that she, Mrs. Portico, might get her out of her troubles. She looked to Georgina, to a considerable degree, to gratify her in this way; but she had really never understood Georgina at all She ought to have been shrewd, but she lacked this refinement, and she never understood anything until after many disappointments and vexations. It was difficult to startle her, but she was much startled by a communication that this young lady made her one fine spring morning. With her florid appearance and her speculative mind, she was probably the most innocent woman in New York.

25

Georgina came very early,—earlier even than visits were paid in New York thirty years ago; and instantly, without any preface, looking her straight in the face, told Mrs. Portico that she was in great trouble and must appeal to her for assistance. Georgina had in her aspect no symptom of distress; she was as fresh and beautiful as the April day itself; she held up her head and smiled, with a sort of familiar bravado, looking like a young woman who would naturally be on good terms with fortune. It was not in the least in the tone of a person making a confession or relating a misadventure that she presently said: "Well, you must know, to begin with—of course, it will surprise you—that I 'm married."

"Married, Georgina Grossie!" Mrs. Portico repeated in her most resonant tones.

Georgina got up, walked with her majestic step across the room, and closed the door. Then she stood there, her back pressed against the mahogany panels, indicating only by the distance she had placed between herself and her hostess the consciousness of an irregular position. "I am not Georgina Gressie! I am Georgina Benyon,—and it has become plain, within a short time, that the natural consequence will take place."

Mrs. Portico was altogether bewildered. "The natural consequence?" she exclaimed, staring.

"Of one's being married, of course,—I suppose you know what that is. No one must know anything about it. I want you to take me to Europe."

Mrs. Portico now slowly rose from her place, and approached her visitor, looking at her from head to foot as she did so, as if to challenge the truth of her remarkable announcement. She rested her hands on Georgina's shoulders a moment, gazing into her blooming face, and then she drew her closer and kissed her. In this way the girl was conducted back to the sofa, where, in a conversation of extreme intimacy, she opened Mrs. Portico's eyes wider than they had ever been opened before. She was Raymond Benyon's wife; they had been married a year, but no one knew anything about it. She had kept it from every one, and she meant to go on keeping it. The ceremony had taken place in a little Episcopal church at Harlem, one Sunday afternoon, after the service.

There was no one in that dusty suburb who knew them; the clergyman, vexed at being detained, and wanting to go home to tea, had made no trouble; he tied the knot before they could turn round. It was ridiculous how easy it had been. Raymond had told him frankly that it must all be under the rose, as the young lady's family disapproved of what she was doing. But she was of legal age, and perfectly free; he could see that for himself. The parson had given a grunt as he looked at her over his spectacles. It was not very complimentary; it seemed to say that she was indeed no chicken. Of course she looked old for a girl; but she was not a girl now, was she? Raymond had certified his own identity as an officer in the United States Navy (he had papers, besides his uniform, which he wore), and introduced the clergyman to a friend he had brought with him, who was also in the navy, a venerable paymaster. It was he who gave Georgina away, as it were; he was an old, old man, a regular grandmother, and perfectly safe. He had been married three times himself. After the ceremony she went back to her father's; but she saw Mr. Benyon the next day. After that, she saw him—for a little while—pretty often. He was always begging her to come to him altogether; she must do him that justice. But she wouldn't—she wouldn't now—perhaps she would n't ever. She had her reasons, which seemed to her very good, but were very difficult to explain. She would tell Mrs. Portico in plenty of time what they were. But that was not the question now, whether they were good or bad; the question was for her to get away from the country for several months,—far away from any one who had ever known her. She would like to go to some little place in Spain or Italy, where she should be out of the world until everything was over.

Mrs. Portico's heart gave a jump as this serene, handsome, familiar girl, sitting there with a hand in hers, and pouring forth this extraordinary tale, spoke of everything being over. There was a glossy coldness in it, an unnatural lightness, which suggested—poor Mrs. Portico scarcely knew what. If Georgina was to become a mother, it was to be supposed she was to remain a mother. She said there was a beautiful place in Italy—Genoa—of which Raymond had often spoken—and where he had been more than once,—he admired it so much; could n't they go there and be quiet for a little while? She was asking a great favor,—that she knew very well; but if Mrs. Portico would n't take her, she would find some one who would. They had talked of such a journey so often; and, certainly, if Mrs. Portico had been willing before, she ought to be much more willing now. The girl declared that she must do something,—go somewhere,—keep, in one way or another, her situation unperceived. There was no use talking to her about telling,—she would rather die than tell. No doubt it seemed strange, but she knew what she was about. No one had guessed anything yet,—she had succeeded perfectly in doing what she wished,—and her father and mother believed—as Mrs. Portico had believed,—had n't she?—that, any time the last year, Raymond Beuyon was less to her than he had been before. Well, so he was; yes, he was. He had gone away—he was off, Heaven knew where—in the Pacific; she was alone, and now she would remain alone. The family believed it was all over,—with his going back to his ship, and other things, and they were right: for it *was* over, or it would be soon.

Mrs. Portico, by this time, had grown almost afraid of her young friend; *she* had so little fear, she had even, as it were, so little shame. If the good lady had been accustomed to analyzing things a little more, she would have said she had so little conscience. She looked at Georgina with dilated eyes,—her visitor was so much the calmer of the two,—and exclaimed, and murmured, and sunk back, and sprung forward, and wiped her forehead with her pocket-handkerchief! There were things she didn't understand; that they should all have been so deceived, that they should have thought Georgina was giving her lover up (they flattered themselves she was discouraged, or had grown tired of him), when she was really only making it impossible she should belong to any one else. And with this, her inconsequence, her capriciousness, her absence of motive, the way she contradicted herself, her apparent belief that she could hush up such a situation forever! There was nothing shameful in having married poor Mr. Benyon, even in a little church at Harlem, and being given away by a paymaster. It was much more shameful to be in such a state without being prepared to make the proper explanations. And she must have seen very little of her husband; she must have given him up—so far as meeting him went—almost as soon as she had taken him. Had not Mrs. Gressie herself told Mrs. Portico (in the preceding October, it must have been) that there now would be no need of sending Georgina away, inasmuch as the affair with the little navy man—a project in every way so unsuitable—had quite blown over?

28

"After our marriage I saw him less, I saw him a great deal less," Georgina explained; but her explanation only appeared to make the mystery more dense.

"I don't see, in that case, what on earth you married him for!"

"We had to be more careful; I wished to appear to have given him up. Of course we were really more intimate,—I saw him differently," Georgina said, smiling.

"I should think so! I can't for the life of me see why you were n't discovered."

"All I can say is we weren't No doubt it's remarkable. We managed very well,—that is, I managed,—he did n't want to manage at all. And then, father and mother are incredibly stupid!"

Mrs. Portico exhaled a comprehensive moan, feeling glad, on the whole, that she had n't a daughter, while Georgina went on to furnish a few more details. Raymond Benyon, in the summer, had been ordered from Brooklyn to Charlestown, near Boston, where, as Mrs. Portico perhaps knew, there was another navy-yard, in which there was a temporary press of work, requiring more oversight He had remained there several months, during which he had written to her urgently to come to him, and during which, as well, he had received notice that he was to rejoin his ship a little later. Before doing so he came back to Brooklyn for a few weeks to wind up his work there, and then she had seen him—well, pretty often. That was the best time of all the year that had elapsed since their marriage. It was a wonder at home that nothing had then been guessed; because she had really been reckless, and Benyon had even tried to force on a disclosure. But they *were* stupid, that was very certain. He had besought her again and again to put an end to their false position, but she did n't want it any more than she had wanted it before. They had rather a bad parting; in fact, for a pair of lovers, it was a very queer parting indeed. He did n't know, now, the thing she had come to tell Mrs. Portico. She had not written to him. He was on a very long cruise. It might be two years before he returned to the United States. "I don't care how long he stays away," Georgina said, very simply.

"You haven't mentioned why you married him. Perhaps you don't remember," Mrs. Portico broke out, with her masculine laugh.

"Oh, yes; I loved him!"

"And you have got over that?"

Georgina hesitated a moment. "Why, no, Mrs. Portico, of course I haven't; Raymond's a splendid fellow."

"Then why don't you live with him? You don't explain that."

"What would be the use when he's always away? How can one live with a man that spends half his life in the South Seas? If he was n't in the navy it would be different; but to go through everything,—I mean everything that making our marriage known would bring upon me,—the scolding and the exposure and the ridicule, the scenes at home,—to go through it all, just for the idea, and yet be alone here, just as I was before, without my husband after all,—with none of the good of him,"—and here Georgina looked at her hostess as if with the certitude that such an enumeration of inconveniences would touch her effectually,—"really, Mrs. Portico, I am bound to say I don't think that would be worth while; I haven't the courage for it."

"I never thought you were a coward," said Mrs. Portico.

"Well, I am not,—if you will give me time. I am very patient."

"I never thought that, either."

"Marrying changes one," said Georgina, still smiling.

"It certainly seems to have had a very peculiar effect upon you. Why don't you make him leave the navy, and arrange your life comfortably, like every one else?"

"I would n't for the world interfere with his prospects—with his promotion. That is sure to come for him, and to come quickly, he has such talents. He is devoted to his profession; it would ruin him to leave it."

"My dear young woman, you are a wonderful creature!" Mrs. Portico exclaimed, looking at her companion as if she had been in a glass case.

"So poor Raymond says," Georgina answered, smiling more than ever.

"Certainly, I should have been very sorry to marry a navy man; but if I had married him, I should stick to him, in the face of all the scoldings in the universe!"

"I don't know what your parents may have been; I know what mine are,", Georgina replied, with some dignity. "When he's a captain, we shall come out of hiding."

"And what shall you do meanwhile? What will you do with your children? Where will you hide them? What will you do with this one?"

Georgina rested her eyes on her lap for a minute; then, raising them, she met those of Mrs. Portico. "Somewhere in Europe," she said, in her sweet tone.

"Georgina Gressie, you 're a monster!" the elder lady cried.

"I know what I am about, and you will help me," the girl went on.

"I will go and tell your father and mother the whole story,—that's what I will do!"

"I am not in the least afraid of that, not in the least. You will help me,—I assure you that you will."

"Do you mean I will support the child?"

Georgina broke into a laugh. "I do believe you would, if I were to ask you! But I won't go so far as that; I have something of my own. All I want you to do is to be with me."

"At Genoa,—yes, you have got it all fixed! You say Mr. Benyon is so fond of the place. That's all very well; but how will he like his infant being deposited there?"

"He won't like it at all. You see I tell you the whole truth," said Georgina, gently.

31

"Much obliged; it's a pity you keep it all for me! It is in his power, then, to make you behave properly. *He* can publish your marriage if you won't; and if he does you will have to acknowledge your child."

"Publish, Mrs. Portico? How little you know my Raymond! He will never break a promise; he will go through fire first."

"And what have you got him to promise?'

"Never to insist on a disclosure against my will; never to claim me openly as his wife till I think it is time; never to let any one know what has passed between us if I choose to keep it still a secret—to keep it for years—to keep it forever. Never to do anything in the matter himself, but to leave it to me. For this he has given me his solemn word of honor. And I know what that means!"

Mrs. Portico, on the sofa, fairly bounded.

"You *do* know what you are about And Mr. Benyon strikes me as more fantastic even than yourself. I never heard of a man taking such an imbecile vow. What good can it do him?"

"What good? The good it did him was that, it gratified me. At the time he took it he would have made any promise under the sun. It was a condition I exacted just at the very last, before the marriage took place. There was nothing at that moment he would have refused me; there was nothing I could n't have made him do. He was in love to that degree—but I don't want to boast," said Georgina, with quiet grandeur. "He wanted—he wanted—" she added; but then she paused.

"He does n't seem to have wanted much!" Mrs. Portico cried, in a tone which made Georgina turn to the window, as if it might have reached the street.

Her hostess noticed the movement and went on: "Oh, my dear, if I ever do tell your story, I will tell it so that people will hear it!"

"You never will tell it. What I mean is, that Raymond wanted the sanction—of the affair at the church—because he saw that I would never do without it. Therefore, for him, the sooner we had it the better, and, to hurry it on, he was ready to take any pledge."

"You have got it pat enough," said Mrs. Portico, in homely phrase. "I don't know what you mean by sanctions, or what *you* wanted of 'em!"

Georgina got up, holding rather higher than before that beautiful head which, in spite of the embarrassments of this interview, had not yet perceptibly abated of its elevation. "Would you have liked me to—to not marry?"

Mrs. Portico rose also, and, flushed with the agitation of unwonted knowledge,—it was as if she had discovered a skeleton in her favorite cupboard,—faced her young friend for a moment. Then her conflicting sentiments resolved themselves into an abrupt question, uttered,—for Mrs. Portico,—with much solemnity: "Georgina Gressie, were you really in love with him?"

The question suddenly dissipated the girl's strange, studied, wilful coldness; she broke out, with a quick flash of passion,—a passion that, for the moment, was predominantly anger, "Why else, in Heaven's name, should I have done what I have done? Why else should I have married him? What under the sun had I to gain?"

A certain quiver in Georgina's voice, a light in her eye which seemed to Mrs. Portico more spontaneous, more human, as she uttered these words, caused them to affect her hostess rather less painfully than anything she had yet said. She took the girl's hand and emitted indefinite, admonitory sounds. "Help me, my dear old friend, help me," Georgina continued, in a low, pleading tone; and in a moment Mrs. Portico saw that the tears were in her eyes.

"You 're a queer mixture, my child," she exclaimed. "Go straight home to your own mother, and tell her everything; that is your best help."

"You are kinder than my mother. You must n't judge her by yourself."

"What can she do to you? How can she hurt you? We are not living in pagan times," said Mrs. Portico, who was seldom so historical "Besides,

33

you have no reason to speak of your mother—to think of her, even—so! She would have liked you to marry a man of some property; but she has always been a good mother to you."

At this rebuke Georgina suddenly kindled again; she was, indeed, as Mrs. Portico had said, a queer mixture. Conscious, evidently, that she could not satisfactorily justify her present stiffness, she wheeled round upon a grievance which absolved her from self-defence. "Why, then, did he make that promise, if he loved me? No man who really loved me would have made it,—and no man that was a man, as I understand being a man! He might have seen that I only did it to test him,—to see if he wanted to take advantage of being left free himself. It is a proof that he does n't love me,—not as he ought to have done; and in such a case as that a woman is n't bound to make sacrifices!"

Mrs. Portico was not a person of a nimble intellect; her mind moved vigorously, but heavily; yet she sometimes made happy guesses. She saw that Georgia's emotions were partly real and partly fictitious; that, as regards this last matter, especially, she was trying to "get up" a resentment, in order to excuse herself. The pretext was absurd, and the good lady was struck with its being heartless on the part of her young visitor to reproach poor Benyon with a concession on which she had insisted, and which could only be a proof of his devotion, inasmuch as he left her free while he bound himself. Altogether, Mrs. Portico was shocked and dismayed at such a want of simplicity in the behavior of a young person whom she had hitherto believed to be as candid as she was elegant, and her appreciation of this discovery expressed itself in the uncompromising remark: "You strike me as a very bad girl, my dear; you strike me as a very bad girl!"

PART II.

III.

It will doubtless seem to the reader very singular that, in spite of this reflection, which appeared to sum up her judgment of the matter, Mrs. Portico should, in the course of a very few days, have consented to everything that Georgina asked of her. I have thought it well to narrate at length the first conversation that took place between them, but I shall not trace further the details of the girl's hard pleading, or the steps by which—in the face of a hundred robust and salutary convictions—the loud, kind, sharp, simple, sceptical, credulous woman took under her protection a damsel whose obstinacy she could not speak of without getting red with anger. It was the simple fact of Georgina's personal condition that moved her; this young lady's greatest eloquence was the seriousness of her predicament She might be bad, and she had a splendid, careless, insolent, fair-faced way of admitting it, which at moments, incoherently, inconsistently, and irresistibly, resolved the harsh confession into tears of weakness; but Mrs. Portico had known her from her rosiest years, and when Georgina declared that she could n't go home, that she wished to be with her and not with her mother, that she could n't expose herself,—how could she?—and that she must remain with her and her only till the day they should sail, the poor lady was forced to make that day a reality. She was overmastered, she was cajoled, she was, to a certain extent, fascinated. She had to accept Georgina's rigidity (she had none of her own to oppose to it; she was only violent, she was not continuous), and once she did this, it was plain, after all, that to take her young friend to Europe was to help her, and to leave her alone was not to help her. Georgina literally frightened Mrs. Portico into compliance. She was evidently capable of strange things if thrown upon her own devices.

So, from one day to another Mrs. Portico announced that she was really at last about to sail for foreign lands (her doctor having told her that if she did n't look out she would get too old to enjoy them), and that she had invited that robust Miss Gressie, who could stand so long on her feet, to accompany her. There was joy in the house of Gressie at this announcement, for though the danger was over, it was a great general advantage to Georgina to go, and the Gressies were always elated at the prospect of an advantage. There was a danger that she might meet Mr. Benyon on the other side of the world; but it didn't seem likely that Mrs. Portico would lend herself to a plot of that kind. If she had taken it into her head to favor their love affair, she would have done it frankly, and Georgina would have been married by this time. Her arrangements were made as quickly as her decision had been—or rather had appeared—slow; for this concerned those agile young men down town. Georgina was perpetually at her house; it was understood in Twelfth Street that she was talking over her future travels with her kind friend. Talk there was, of course to a considerable degree; but after it was settled they should start nothing more was said about the motive of the journey. Nothing was said, that is, till the night before they sailed; then a few words passed between them. Georgina had already taken leave of her relations in Twelfth Street, and was to sleep at Mrs. Portico's in order to go down to the ship at an early hour. The two ladies were sitting together in the firelight, silent, with the consciousness of corded luggage, when the elder one suddenly remarked to her companion that she seemed to be taking a great deal upon herself in assuming that Raymond Benyon wouldn't force her hand. *He* might choose to acknowledge his child, if she didn't; there were promises and promises, and many people would consider they had been let off when circumstances were so altered. She would have to reckon with Mr. Benyon more than she thought.

"I know what I am about," Georgina answered. "There is only one promise, for him. I don't know what you mean by circumstances being altered."

"Everything seems to me to be changed," poor Mrs. Portico murmured, rather tragically.

"Well, he is n't, and he never will! I am sure of him,—as sure as that I sit here. Do you think I would have looked at him if I had n't known he was a man of his word?"

"You have chosen him well, my dear," said Mrs. Portico, who by this time was reduced to a kind of bewildered acquiescence.

"Of course I have chosen him well! In such a matter as this he will be perfectly splendid." Then suddenly, "Perfectly splendid,—that's why I cared for him!" she repeated, with a flash of incongruous passion.

This seemed to Mrs. Portico audacious to the point of being sublime; but she had given up trying to understand anything that the girl might say or do. She understood less and less, after they had disembarked in England and begun to travel southward; and she understood least of all when, in the middle of the winter, the event came off with which, in imagination, she had tried to familiarize herself, but which, when it occurred, seemed to her beyond measure strange and dreadful. It took place at Genoa, for Georgina had made up her mind that there would be more privacy in a big town than in a little; and she wrote to America that both Mrs. Portico and she had fallen in love with the place and would spend two or three months there. At that time people in the United States knew much less than to-day about the comparative attractions of foreign cities, and it was not thought surprising that absent New Yorkers should wish to linger in a seaport where they might find apartments, according to Georgina's report, in a palace painted in fresco by Vandyke and Titian. Georgina, in her letters, omitted, it will be seen, no detail that could give color to Mrs. Portico's long stay at Genoa. In such a palace—where the travellers hired twenty gilded rooms for the most insignificant sum—a remarkably fine boy came into the world. Nothing could have been more successful and comfortable than this transaction. Mrs. Portico was almost appalled at the facility and felicity of it. She was by this time in a pretty bad way, and—what had never happened to her before in her life—she suffered from chronic depression of spirits. She hated to have to lie, and now she was lying all the time. Everything she wrote home, everything that had been said or done in connection with their stay in Genoa, was a lie. The way they remained indoors to avoid meeting chance compatriots was a lie. Compatriots, in Genoa, at that period, were very rare; but nothing could exceed the businesslike completeness of Georgina's precautions. Her nerves, her self-possession, her apparent want of feeling, excited on Mrs. Portico's part a kind of gloomy suspense; a morbid anxiety to see how far her companion would go took possession of the excellent woman, who, a few months before, hated to fix her mind on disagreeable things.

Georgina went very far indeed; she did everything in her power to dissimulate the origin of her child. The record of its birth was made under a false name, and he was baptized at the nearest church by a Catholic priest. A magnificent contadina was brought to light by the doctor in a village in the hills, and this big, brown, barbarous creature, who, to do her justice, was full of handsome, familiar smiles and coarse tenderness, was constituted nurse to Raymond Benyon's son. She nursed him for a fortnight under the mother's eye, and she was then sent back to her village with the baby in her arms and sundry gold coin knotted into a corner of her rude pocket-handkerchief. Mr. Gressie had given his daughter a liberal letter of credit on a London banker, and she was able, for the present, to make abundant provision for the little one. She called Mrs. Portico's attention to the fact that she spent none of her money on futilities; she kept it all for her small pensioner in the Genoese hills. Mrs. Portico beheld these strange doings with a stupefaction that occasionally broke into passionate protest; then she relapsed into a brooding sense of having now been an accomplice so far that she must be an accomplice to the end. The two ladies went down to Rome—Georgina was in wonderful trim—to finish the season, and here Mrs. Portico became convinced that she intended to abandon her offspring. She had not driven into the country to see the nursling before leaving Genoa,—she had said that she could n't bear to see it in such a place and among such people. Mrs. Portico, it must be added, had felt the force of this plea,—felt it as regards a plan of her own, given up after being hotly entertained for a few hours, of devoting a day, by herself, to a visit to the big contadina. It seemed to her that if she should see the child in the sordid hands to which Georgina had consigned it she would become still more of a participant than she was already. This young woman's blooming hardness, after they got to Borne, acted upon her like a kind of Medusa-mask. She had seen a horrible thing, she had been mixed up with it, and her motherly heart had received a mortal chill. It became more clear to her every day that, though Georgina would continue to send the infant money in considerable quantities, she had dispossessed herself of it forever. Together with this induction a fixed idea settled in her mind,—the project of taking the baby herself, of making him her own, of arranging that matter with the father. The countenance she had given Georgina up to this point was an effective pledge that she would not expose her; but she could adopt the child without exposing her; she could say that he was a lovely baby—he was lovely, fortunately—whom she had picked up in a poor village in Italy,—a village that had been devastated by brigands. She would pretend—she could pretend; oh, yes, of course, she could pretend! Everything was imposture now, and she could go on to lie as she had begun. The falsity of the whole business sickened her; it made her so yellow that she scarcely knew herself in her glass. None the less, to rescue the child, even if she had to become falser still, would be in some measure an atonement for the treachery to which she had already lent herself. She began to hate Georgina, who had drawn her into such an atrocious current, and if it had not been for two considerations she would have insisted on their separating. One was the deference she owed to Mr. and Mrs. Gressie, who had reposed such a trust in her; the other was that she must keep hold of the mother till she had got possession of the infant Meanwhile, in this forced communion, her aversion to her companion increased; Georgina came to appear to her a creature of brass, of iron; she was exceedingly afraid of her, and it seemed to her now a wonder of wonders that she should ever have trusted her enough to come so far. Georgina showed no consciousness of the change in Mrs. Portico, though there was, indeed, at present, not even a pretence of confidence between the two. Miss Gressie—that was another lie, to which Mrs. Portico had to lend herself—was bent on enjoying Europe, and was especially delighted with Rome. She certainly had the courage of her undertaking, and she confessed to Mrs. Portico that she had left Raymond Benyon, and meant to continue to leave him, in ignorance of what had taken place at Genoa. There was a certain confidence, it must be said, in that. He was now in Chinese waters, and she probably should not see him for years.

Mrs. Portico took counsel with herself, and the result of her cogitation was, that she wrote to Mr. Benyon that a charming little boy had been born to him, and that Georgina had put him to nurse with Italian peasants, but that, if he would kindly consent to it, she, Mrs. Portico, would bring him up much better than that. She knew not how to address her letter, and Georgina, even if *she* should know, which was doubtful, would never tell her; so she sent the missive to the care of the Secretary of the Navy, at Washington, with an earnest request that it might immediately be forwarded. Such was Mrs. Portico's last effort in this strange business of Georgina's. I relate rather a complicated fact in a very few words when I say that the poor lady's anxieties, indignations, repentances, preyed upon her until they fairly broke her down. Various persons whom she knew in Borne notified her that the air of the Seven Hills was plainly unfavorable to her, and she had made up her mind to return to her native land, when she found that, in her depressed condition, malarial fever had laid its hand upon her. She was unable to move, and the matter was settled for her in the course of an illness which, happily, was not prolonged. I have said that she was not obstinate, and the resistance that she made on the present occasion was not worthy even of her spasmodic energy. Brain-fever made its appearance, and she died at the end of three weeks, during which Georgina's attentions to her patient and protectress had been unremitting. There were other Americans in Rome who, after this sad event, extended to the bereaved young lady every comfort and hospitality. She had no lack of opportunities for returning under a proper escort to New York. She selected, you may be sure, the best, and re-entered her father's house, where she took to plain dressing; for she sent all her pocket-money, with the utmost secrecy, to the little boy in the Genoese hills.

IV.

"Why should he come if he doesn't like you? He is under no obligation, and he has his ship to look after. Why should he sit for an hour at a time, and why should he be so pleasant?"

"Do you think he is very pleasant?" Kate Theory asked, turning away her face from her sister. It was important that Mildred should not see how little the expression of that charming countenance corresponded with the inquiry.

This precaution was useless, however, for in a moment Mildred said, from the delicately draped couch, where she lay at the open window, "Kate Theory, don't be affected!"

"Perhaps it's for you he comes. I don't see why he should n't; you are far more attractive than I, and you have a great deal more to say. How can he help seeing that you are the cleverest of the clever? You can talk to him of everything: of the dates of the different eruptions, of the statues and bronzes in the Museum, which you have never seen, poor darling! but which you know more about than he does, than any one does. What was it you began on last time? Oh, yes, you poured forth floods about Magna Græcia. And then—and then—" But with this Kate Theory paused; she felt it would n't do to speak the words that had risen to her lips. That her sister was as beautiful as a saint, and as delicate and refined as an angel,—she had been on the point of saying something of that sort But Mildred's beauty and delicacy were the fairness of mortal disease, and to praise her for her refinement was simply to intimate that she had the tenuity of a consumptive. So, after she had checked herself, the younger girl—she was younger only by a year or two—simply kissed her tenderly, and settled the knot of the lace handkerchief that was tied over her head. Mildred knew what she had been going to say,—knew why she had stopped. Mildred knew everything, without ever leaving her room, or leaving, at least, that little salon of their own, at the *pension*, which she had made so pretty by simply lying there, at the window that had the view of the bay and of Vesuvius, and telling Kate how to arrange and rearrange everything. Since it began to be plain that Mildred must spend her small remnant of years altogether in warm climates, the lot of the two sisters had been cast in the ungarnished hostelries of southern Europe. Their little sitting-room was sure to be very ugly, and Mildred was never happy till it was rearranged. Her sister fell to work, as a matter of course, the first day, and changed the place of all the tables, sofas, chairs, till every combination had been tried, and the invalid thought at last that there was a little effect Kate Theory had a taste of her own, and her ideas were not always the same as her sister's; but she did whatever Mildred liked, and if the poor girl had told her to put the doormat on the dining-table, or the clock under the sofa, she would have obeyed without a murmur. Her own ideas, her personal tastes, had been folded up and put away, like garments out of season, in drawers and trunks, with camphor and lavender. They were not, as a general thing, for southern wear, however indispensable to comfort in the climate of New England, where poor Mildred had lost her health. Kate Theory, ever since this event, had lived for her companion, and it was almost an inconvenience for her to think that she was attractive to Captain Benyon. It was as if she had shut up her house and was not in a position to entertain. So long as Mildred should live, her own life was suspended; if there should be any time afterwards, perhaps she would take it up again; but for the present, in answer to any knock at her door, she could only call down from one of her dusty windows that she was not at home. Was it really in these terms she should have to dismiss Captain Benyon? If Mildred said it was for her he came she must perhaps take upon herself such a duty; for, as we have seen, Mildred knew everything, and she must therefore be right She knew about the statues in the Museum, about the excavations at Pompeii, about the antique splendor of Magna Græcia. She always had some instructive volume on the table beside her sofa, and she had strength enough to hold the book for half an hour at a time. That was about the only strength she had now. The Neapolitan winters had been remarkably soft, but after the first month or two she had been obliged to give up her little walks in the garden. It lay beneath her window like a single enormous bouquet; as early as May, that year, the flowers were so dense. None of them, however, had a color so intense as the splendid blue of the bay, which filled up all the rest of the view. It would have looked painted, if you had not been able to see the little movement of the waves. Mildred Theory watched them by the hour, and the breathing crest of the volcano, on the other side of Naples, and the great sea-vision of Capri, on the horizon, changing its tint while her eyes rested there, and wondered what would become of her sister after she was gone. Now that Percival was married,—he was their only brother, and from one day to the other was to come down to Naples to show them his new wife, as yet a complete stranger, or revealed only in the few letters she had written them during her wedding tour,—now that Percival was to be quite taken up, poor Kate's situation would be much more grave. Mildred felt that she should be able to judge better, after she should have seen her sister-in-law, how much of a home Kate might expect to find with the pair; but even if Agnes should prove—well, more satisfactory than her letters, it was a wretched prospect for Kate,—this living as a mere appendage to happier people. Maiden aunts were very well, but being a maiden aunt was only a last resource, and Kate's first resources had not even been tried.

Meanwhile the latter young lady wondered as well,—wondered in what book Mildred had read that Captain Benyon was in love with her. She admired him, she thought, but he didn't seem a man that would fall in love with one like that She could see that he was on his guard; he would n't throw himself away. He thought too much of himself, or at any rate he took too good care of himself,—in the manner of a man to whom something had happened which had given him a lesson. Of course what had happened was that his heart was buried somewhere,—in some woman's grave; he had loved some beautiful girl,—much more beautiful, Kate was sure, than she, who thought herself small and dark,—and the maiden had died, and his capacity to love had died with her. He loved her memory,—that was the only thing he would care for now. He was quiet, gentle, clever, humorous, and very kind in his manner; but if any one save Mildred had said to her that if he came three times a week to Posilippo, it was for anything but to pass his time (he had told them he didn't know another soul in Naples), she would have felt that this was simply the kind of thing—usually so idiotic—that people always thought it necessary to say. It was very easy for him to come; he had the big ship's boat, with nothing else to do; and what could be more delightful than to be rowed across the bay, under a bright awning, by four brown sailors with "Louisiana" in blue letters on their immaculate white shirts, and in gilt letters on their fluttering hat ribbons? The boat came to the steps of the garden of the *pension*, where the orange-trees hung over and made vague yellow balls shine back out of the water. Kate Theory knew all about that, for Captain Benyon had persuaded her to take a turn in the boat, and if they had only had another lady to go with them, he could have conveyed her to the ship, and shown her all over it It looked beautiful, just a little way off, with the American flag hanging loose in the Italian air. They would have another lady when Agnes should arrive; then Percival would remain with Mildred while they took this excursion. Mildred had stayed alone the day she went in the boat; she had insisted on it, and, of course it was really Mildred who had persuaded her; though now that Kate came to think of it, Captain Benyon had, in his quiet, waiting way—he turned out to be waiting long after you thought he had let a thing pass—said a good deal about the pleasure it would give him. Of course, everything would give pleasure to a man who was so bored. He was keeping the "Louisiana" at Naples, week after week, simply because these were the commodore's orders. There was no work to be done there, and his time was on his hands; but of course the commodore, who had gone to Constantinople with the two other ships, had to be obeyed to the letter, however mysterious his motives. It made no difference that he was a fantastic, grumbling, arbitrary old commodore; only a good while afterwards it occurred to Kate Theory that, for a reserved, correct man, Captain Benyon had given her a considerable proof of confidence, in speaking to her in these terms of his superior officer. If he looked at all hot when he arrived at the *pension*, she offered him a glass of cold "orangeade." Mildred thought this an unpleasant drink,—she called it messy; but Kate adored it, and Captain Benyon always accepted it.

The day I speak of, to change the subject, she called her sister's attention to the extraordinary sharpness of a zigzagging cloud-shadow, on the tinted slope of Vesuvius; but Mildred only remarked in answer that she wished her sister would many the captain. It was in this familiar way that constant meditation led Miss Theory to speak of him; it shows how constantly she thought of him, for, in general, no one was more ceremonious than she, and the failure of her health had not caused her to relax any form that it was possible to keep up. There was a kind of slim erectness, even in the way she lay on her sofa; and she always received the doctor as if he were calling for the first time.

"I had better wait till he asks me," Kate Theory said. "Dear Milly, if I were to do some of the things you wish me to do, I should shock you very much."

"I wish he would marry you, then. You know there is very little time, if I wish to see it."

"You will never see it, Mildred. I don't see why you should take so for granted that I would accept him."

"You will never meet a man who has so few disagreeable qualities. He is probably not enormously rich. I don't know what is the pay of a captain in the navy—"

"It's a relief to find there is something you don't know," Kate Theory broke in.

"But when I am gone," her sister went on calmly, "when I am gone there will be plenty for both of you."

The younger sister, at this, was silent for a moment; then she exclaimed, "Mildred, you may be out of health, but I don't see why you should be dreadful!"

"You know that since we have been leading this life we have seen no one we liked better," said Milly. When she spoke of the life they were leading—there was always a soft resignation of regret and contempt in the allusion—she meant the southern winters, the foreign climates, the vain experiments, the lonely waitings, the wasted hours, the interminable rains, the bad food, the pottering, humbugging doctors, the damp *pensions*, the chance encounters, the fitful apparitions, of fellow-travellers.

"Why should n't you speak for yourself alone? I am glad *you* like him, Mildred."

"If you don't like him, why do you give him orangeade?"

At this inquiry Kate began to laugh, and her sister continued,—

"Of course you are glad I like him, my dear. If I did n't like him, and you did, it would n't be satisfactory at all. I can imagine nothing more miserable; I should n't die in any sort of comfort."

Kate Theory usually checked this sort of allusion—she was always too late—with a kiss; but on this occasion she added that it was a long time since Mildred had tormented her so much as she had done to-day. "You will make me hate him," she added.

"Well, that proves you don't already," Milly rejoined; and it happened that almost at this moment they saw, in the golden afternoon, Captain Benyon's boat approaching the steps at the end of the garden. He came that day, and he came two days later, and he came yet once again after an interval equally brief, before Percival Theory arrived, with Mrs. Percival, from Borne. He seemed anxious to crowd into these few days, as he would have said, a good deal of intercourse with the two remarkably nice girls—or nice women, he hardly knew which to call them—whom in the course of a long, idle, rather tedious detention at Naples, he had discovered in the lovely suburb of Posilippo. It was the American consul who had put him into relation with them; the sisters had had to sign, in the consul's presence, some law-papers, transmitted to them by the man of business who looked after their little property in America, and the kindly functionary, taking advantage of the pretext (Captain Benyon happened to come into the consulate as he was starting, indulgently, to wait upon the ladies) to bring together "two parties" who, as he said, ought to appreciate each other, proposed to his fellow-officer in the service of the United States that he should go with him as witness of the little ceremony. He might, of course, take his clerk, but the captain would do much better; and he represented to Benyon that the Miss Theorys (singular name, wa' n't it?) suffered—he was sure—from a lack of society; also that one of them was very sick, that they were real pleasant and extraordinarily refined, and that the sight of a compatriot, literally draped, as it were, in the national banner, would cheer them up more than most anything, and give them a sense of protection. They had talked to the consul about Benyon's ship, which they could see from their windows, in the distance, at its anchorage. They were the only American ladies then at Naples,—the only residents, at least,—and the captain would n't be doing the polite thing unless he went to pay them his respects. Benyon felt afresh how little it was in his line to call upon strange women; he was not in the habit of hunting up female acquaintance, or of looking out for the soft emotions which the sex only can inspire. He had his reasons for this abstention, and he seldom relaxed it; but the consul appealed to him on rather strong grounds; and he suffered himself to be persuaded. He was far from regretting, during the first weeks at least, an act which was distinctly inconsistent with his great rule,—that of never exposing himself to the chance of seriously caring for an unmarried woman. He had been obliged to make this rule, and had adhered to it with some success. He was fond of women, but he was forced to restrict himself to superficial sentiments. There was no use tumbling into situations from which the only possible issue was a retreat The step he had taken with regard to poor Miss Theory and her delightful little sister was an exception on which at first he could only congratulate himself. That had been a happy idea of the ruminating old consul; it made Captain Benyon forgive him his hat, his boots, his shirtfront,—a costume which might be considered representative, and the effect of which was to make the observer turn with rapture to a half-naked lazzarone. On either side the acquaintance had helped the time to pass, and the hours he spent at the little *pension* at Posilippo left a sweet—and by no means innutritive—taste behind.

As the weeks went by his exception had grown to look a good deal like a rule; but he was able to remind himself that the path of retreat was always open to him. Moreover, if he should fall in love with the younger girl there would be no great harm, for Kate Theory was in love only with her sister, and it would matter very little to her whether he advanced or retreated. She was very attractive, or rather very attracting. Small, pale, attentive without rigidity, full of pretty curves and quick movements, she looked as if the habit of watching and serving had taken complete possession of her, and was literally a little sister of charity. Her thick black hair was pushed behind her ears, as if to help her to listen, and her clear brown eyes had the smile of a person too full of tact to cany a dull face to a sickbed. She spoke in an encouraging voice, and had soothing and unselfish habits. She was very pretty,—producing a cheerful effect of contrasted black and white, and dressed herself daintily, so that Mildred might have something agreeable to look at Benyon very soon perceived that there was a fund of good service in her. Her sister had it all now; but poor Miss Theory was fading fast, and then what would become of this precious little force? The answer to such a question that seemed most to the point was that it was none of his business. He was not sick,—at least not physically,—and he was not looking out for a nurse. Such a companion might be a luxury, but was not, as yet, a necessity: The welcome of the two ladies, at first, had been simple, and he scarcely knew what to call it but sweet; a bright, gentle friendliness remained the tone of their greeting. They evidently liked him to come,—they liked to see his big transatlantic ship hover about those gleaming coasts of exile. The fact of Miss Mildred being always stretched on her couch—in his successive visits to foreign waters Benyon had not unlearned (as why should he?) the pleasant American habit of using the lady's personal name—made their intimacy seem greater, their differences less; it was as if his hostesses had taken him into their confidence and he had been—as the consul would have said—of the same party. Knocking about the salt parts of the globe, with a few feet square on a rolling frigate for his only home, the pretty, flower-decked sitting-room of the quiet American sisters became, more than anything he had hitherto known, his interior. He had dreamed once of having an interior, but the dream had vanished in lurid smoke, and no such vision had come to him again. He had a feeling that the end of this was drawing nigh; he was sure that the advent of the strange brother, whose wife was certain to be disagreeable, would make a difference. That is why, as I have said, he came as often as possible the last week, after he had learned the day on which Percival Theory would arrive. The limits of the exception had been reached.

He had been new to the young ladies at Posilippo, and there was no reason why they should say to each other that he was a very different man from the ingenuous youth who, ten years before, used to wander with Georgina Gressie down vistas of plank fences brushed over with the advertisements of quack medicines. It was natural he should be, and we, who know him, would have found that he had traversed the whole scale of alteration. There was nothing ingenuous in him now; he had the look of experience, of having been seasoned and hardened by the years.

His face, his complexion, were the same; still smooth-shaven and slim, he always passed, at first, for a man scarcely out of his twenties. But his expression was old, and his talk was older still,—the talk of one who had seen much of the world (as indeed he had, to-day), and judged most things for himself, with a humorous scepticism which, whatever concessions it might make, superficially, for the sake of not offending (for instance) two remarkably nice American women, of the kind that had kept most of their illusions, left you with the conviction that the next minute it would go quickly back to its own standpoint There was a curious contradiction in him; he struck you as serious, and yet he could not be said to take things seriously. This was what made Kate Theory feel so sure that he had lost the object of his affections; and she said to herself that it must have been under circumstances of peculiar sadness, for that was, after all, a frequent accident, and was not usually thought, in itself, a sufficient stroke to make a man a cynic. This reflection, it may be added, was, on the young lady's part, just the least bit acrimonious. Captain Benyon was not a cynic in any sense in which he might have shocked an innocent mind; he kept his cynicism to himself, and was a very clever, courteous, attentive gentleman. If he was melancholy, you knew it chiefly by his jokes, for they were usually at his own expense; and if he was indifferent, it was all the more to his credit that he should have exerted himself to entertain his countrywomen.

The last time he called before the arrival of the expected brother, he found Miss Theory alone, and sitting up, for a wonder, at her window. Kate had driven into Naples to give orders at the hotel for the reception of the travellers, who required accommodation more spacious than the villa at Posilippo (where the two sisters had the best rooms) could offer them; and the sick girl had taken advantage of her absence and of the pretext afforded by a day of delicious warmth, to transfer herself, for the first time in six months, to an arm-chair. She was practising, as she said, for the long carriage-journey to the north, where, in a quiet corner they knew of, on the Lago Maggiore, her summer was to be spent. Eaymond Benyon remarked to her that she had evidently turned the corner and was going to get well, and this gave her a chance to say various things that were on her mind. She had many things on her mind, poor Mildred Theory, so caged and restless, and yet so resigned and patient as she was; with a clear, quick spirit, in the most perfect health, ever reaching forward, to the end of its tense little chain, from her wasted and suffering body; and, in the course of the perfect summer afternoon, as she sat there, exhilarated by the success of her effort to get up, and by her comfortable opportunity, she took her friendly visitor into the confidence of most of her anxieties. She told him, very promptly and positively, that she was not going to get well at all, that she had probably not more than ten months yet to live, and that he would oblige her very much by not forcing her to waste any more breath in contradicting him on that point. Of course she could n't talk much; therefore, she wished to say to him only things that he would not hear from any one else. Such, for instance, was her present secret—Katie's and hers—the secret of their fearing so much that they should n't like Percival's wife, who was not from Boston, but from New York. Naturally, that by itself would be nothing, but from what they had heard of her set—this subject had been explored by their correspondents—they were rather nervous, nervous to the point of not being in the least reassured by the fact that the young lady would bring Percival a fortune. The fortune was a matter of course, for that was just what they had heard about Agnes's circle—that the stamp of money was on all their thoughts and doings. They were very rich and very new and very splashing, and evidently had very little in common with the two Miss Theorys, who, moreover, if the truth must be told (and this was a great secret), did not care much for the letters their sister-in-law had hitherto addressed them. She had been at a French boarding-school in New York, and yet (and this was the greatest secret of all) she wrote to them that she had performed a part of the journey through France in *diligance!*

Of course, they would see the next day; Miss Mildred was sure she should know in a moment whether Agnes would like them. She could never have told him all this if her sister had been there, and Captain Benyon must promise never to reveal to Kate how she had chattered. Kate thought always that they must hide everything, and that even if Agnes should be a dreadful disappointment they must never let any one guess it And yet Kate was just the one who would suffer, in the coming years, after she herself had gone. Their brother had been everything to them, but now it would all be different Of course it was not to be expected that he should have remained a bachelor for their sake; she only wished he had waited till she was dead and Kate was married One of these events, it was true, was much less sure than the other; Kate might never marry,—much as she wished she would! She was quite morbidly unselfish, and did n't think she had a right to have anything of her own—not even a husband. Miss Mildred talked a good while about Kate, and it never occurred to her that she might bore Captain Benyon. She did n't, in point of fact; he had none of the trouble of wondering why this poor, sick, worried lady was trying to push her sister down his throat Their peculiar situation made everything natural, and the tone she took with him now seemed only what their pleasant relation for the last three months led up to. Moreover, he had an excellent reason for not being bored: the fact, namely, that after all, with regard to her sister, Miss Mildred appeared to him to keep back more than she uttered. She didn't tell him the great thing,— she had nothing to say as to what that charming girl thought of Eaymond Benyon. The effect of their interview, indeed, was to make him shrink from knowing, and he felt that the right thing for him would be to get back into his boat, which was waiting at the garden steps, before Kate Theory should return from Naples. It came over him, as he sat there, that he was far too interested in knowing what this young lady thought of him. She might think what she pleased; it could make no difference to him. The best opinion in the world—if it looked out at him from her tender eyes—would not make him a whit more free or more happy. Women of that sort were not for him, women whom one could not see familiarly without falling in love with them, and whom it was no use to fall in love with unless one was ready to marry them. The light of the summer afternoon, and of Miss Mildred's pure spirit, seemed suddenly to flood the whole subject. He saw that he was in danger, and he had long since made up his mind that from this particular peril it was not only necessary but honorable to flee. He took leave of his hostess before her sister reappeared, and had the courage even to say to her that he would not come back often after that; they would be so much occupied by their brother and his wife! As he moved across the glassy bay, to the rhythm of the oars, he wished either that the sisters would leave Naples or that his confounded commodore would send for him.

When Kate returned from her errand, ten minutes later, Milly told her of the captain's visit, and added that she had never seen anything so sudden as the way he left her. "He would n't wait for you, my dear, and he said he thought it more than likely that he should never see us again. It is as if he thought you were going to die too!"

"Is his ship called away?" Kate Theory asked.

"He did n't tell me so; he said we should be so busy with Percival and Agnes."

"He has got tired of us,—that's all. There's nothing wonderful in that; I knew he would."

Mildred said nothing for a moment; she was watching her sister, who was very attentively arranging some flowers. "Yes, of course, we are very dull, and he is like everybody else."

"I thought you thought he was so wonderful," said Kate, "and so fond of us."

"So he is; I am surer of that than ever. That's why he went away so abruptly."

Kate looked at her sister now. "I don't understand."

"Neither do I, darling. But you will, one of these days."

"How if he never comes back?"

"Oh, he will—after a while—when I am gone. Then he will explain; that, at least, is clear to me."

"My poor precious, as if I cared!" Kate Theory exclaimed, smiling as she distributed her flowers. She carried them to the window, to place them near her sister, and here she paused a moment, her eye caught by an object, far out in the bay, with which she was not unfamiliar. Mildred noticed its momentary look, and followed its direction.

"It's the captain's gig going back to the ship," Milly said. "It's so still one can almost hear the oars."

Kate Theory turned away, with a sudden, strange violence, a movement and exclamation which, the very next minute, as she became conscious of what she had said,—and, still more, of what she felt—smote her own heart (as it flushed her face) with surprise, and with the force of a revelation: "I wish it would sink him to the bottom of the sea!"

Her sister stared, then caught her by the dress, as she passed from her, drawing her back with a weak hand. "Oh, my dearest, my poorest!" And she pulled Kate down and down toward her, so that the girl had nothing for it but to sink on her knees and bury her face in Mildred's lap. If that ingenious invalid did not know everything now, she knew a great deal.

PART III.

V.

Mrs. Percival proved very pretty. It is more gracious to begin with this declaration, instead of saying that, in the first place, she proved very silly. It took a long day to arrive at the end of her silliness, and the two ladies at Posilippo, even after a week had passed, suspected that they had only skirted its edges. Kate Theory had not spent half an hour in her company before she gave a little private sigh of relief; she felt that a situation which had promised to be embarrassing was now quite clear, was even of a primitive simplicity. She would spend with her sister-in-law, in the coming time, one week in the year; that was all that was mortally possible. It was a blessing that one could see exactly what she was, for in that way the question settled itself. It would have been much more tiresome if Agnes had been a little less obvious; then she would have had to hesitate and consider and weigh one thing against another. She was pretty and silly, as distinctly as an orange is yellow and round; and Kate Theory would as soon have thought of looking to her to give interest to the future as she would have thought of looking to an orange to impart solidity to the prospect of dinner. Mrs. Percival travelled in the hope of meeting her American acquaintance, or of making acquaintance with such Americans as she did meet, and for the purpose of buying mementos for her relations. She was perpetually adding to her store of articles in tortoise-shell, in mother-of-pearl, in olive-wood, in ivory, in filigree, in tartan lacquer, in mosaic; and she had a collection of Roman scarfs and Venetian beads, which she looked over exhaustively every night before she went to bed. Her conversation bore mainly upon the manner in which she intended to dispose of these accumulations. She was constantly changing about, among each other, the persons to whom they were respectively to be offered. At Borne one of the first things she said to her husband after entering the Coliseum had been: "I guess I will give the ivory work-box to Bessie and the Roman pearls to

Aunt Harriet!" She was always hanging over the travellers' book at the hotel; she had it brought up to her, with a cup of chocolate, as soon as she arrived. She searched its pages for the magical name of New York, and she indulged in infinite conjecture as to who the people were—the name was sometimes only a partial cue—who had inscribed it there. What she most missed in Europe, and what she most enjoyed, were the New Yorkers; when she met them she talked about the people in their native city who had "moved" and the streets they had moved to. "Oh, yes, the Drapers are going up town, to Twenty-fourth Street, and the Vanderdeckens are going to be in Twenty-third Street, right back of them. My uncle, Henry Piatt, thinks of building round there." Mrs. Percival Theory was capable of repeating statements like these thirty times over,—of lingering on them for hours. She talked largely of herself, of her uncles and aunts, of her clothes—past, present, and future. These articles, in especial, filled her horizon; she considered them with a complacency which might have led you to suppose that she had invented the custom of draping the human form. Her main point of contact with Naples was the purchase of coral; and all the while she was there the word "set"—she used it as if every one would understand—fell with its little, flat, common sound upon the ears of her sisters-in-law, who had no sets of anything. She cared little for pictures and mountains; Alps and Apennines were not productive of New Yorkers, and it was difficult to take an interest in Madonnas who flourished at periods when, apparently, there were no fashions, or, at any rate, no trimmings.

I speak here not only of the impression she made upon her husband's anxious sisters, but of the judgment passed on her (he went so far as that, though it was not obvious how it mattered to him) by Raymond Benyon. And this brings me at a jump (I confess it's a very small one) to the fact that he did, after all, go back to Posilippo. He stayed away for nine days, and at the end of this time Percival Theory called upon him, to thank him for the civility he had shown his kinswomen. He went to this gentleman's hotel, to return his visit, and there he found Miss Kate, in her brother's sitting-room. She had come in by appointment from the villa, and was going with the others to seek the royal palace, which she had not yet had an opportunity to inspect It was proposed (not by Kate), and presently arranged, that Captain Benyon should go with them, and he accordingly walked over marble floors for half an hour, exchanging conscious commonplaces with the woman he loved. For this truth had rounded itself during those nine days of absence; he discovered that there was nothing particularly sweet in his life when once Kate Theory had been excluded from it He had stayed away to keep himself from falling in love with her; but this expedient was in itself illuminating, for he perceived that, according to the vulgar adage, he was locking the stable door after the horse had been stolen. As he paced the deck of his ship and looked toward Posilippo, his tenderness crystallized; the thick, smoky flame of a sentiment that knew itself forbidden and was angry at the knowledge, now danced upon the fuel of his good resolutions. The latter, it must be said, resisted, declined to be consumed. He determined that he would see Kate Theory again, for a time, just sufficient to bid her good-by, and to add a little explanation. He thought of his explanation very lovingly, but it may not strike the reader as a happy inspiration. To part from her dryly, abruptly, without an allusion to what he might have said if everything had been different,—that would be wisdom, of course, that would be virtue, that would be the line of a practical man, of a man who kept himself well in hand. But it would be virtue terribly unrewarded,—it would be virtue too austere for a person who sometimes flattered himself that he had taught himself stoicism. The minor luxury tempted him irresistibly, since the larger—that of happy love—was denied him; the luxury of letting the girl know that it would not be an accident—oh, not at all—that they should never meet again. She might easily think it was, and thinking it was would doubtless do her no harm. But this would n't give him his pleasure,—the Platonic satisfaction of expressing to her at the same time his belief that they might have made each other happy, and the necessity of his renunciation. That, probably, wouldn't hurt her either, for she had given him no proof whatever that she cared for him. The nearest approach to it was the way she walked beside him now, sweet and silent, without the least reference to his not having been back to the villa. The place was cool and dusky, the blinds were drawn, to keep out the light and noise, and the little party wandered through the high saloons, where precious marbles and the gleam of gilding and satin made reflections in the rich dimness. Here and there the cicerone, in slippers, with Neapolitan familiarity, threw open a shutter to show off a picture on a tapestry. He strolled in front with Percival

Theory and his wife, while this lady, drooping silently from her husband's arm as they passed, felt the stuff of the curtains and the sofas. When he caught her in these experiments, the cicerone, in expressive deprecation, clasped his hands and lifted his eyebrows; whereupon Mrs. Theory exclaimed to her husband, "Oh, bother his old king!" It was not striking to Captain Benyon why Percival Theory had married the niece of Mr. Henry Piatt. He was less interesting than his sisters,—a smooth, cool, correct young man, who frequently took out a pencil and did a little arithmetic on the back of a letter. He sometimes, in spite of his correctness, chewed a toothpick, and he missed the American papers, which he used to ask for in the most unlikely places. He was a Bostonian converted to New York; a very special type.

"Is it settled when you leave Naples?" Benyon asked of Kate Theory.

"I think so; on the twenty-fourth. My brother has been very kind; he has lent us his carriage, which is a large one, so that Mildred can lie down. He and Agnes will take another; but, of course, we shall travel together."

"I wish to Heaven I were going with you?" Captain Benyon said. He had given her the opportunity to respond, but she did not take it; she merely remarked, with a vague laugh, that of course he couldn't take his ship over the Apennines. "Yes, there is always my ship," he went on. "I am afraid that in future it will carry me far away from you."

They were alone in one of the royal apartments; their companions had passed, in advance of them, into the adjoining room. Benyon and his fellow-visitor had paused beneath one of the immense chandeliers of glass, which in the clear, colored gloom (through it one felt the strong outer light of Italy beating in) suspended its twinkling drops from the decorated vault. They looked round them confusedly, made shy for the moment by Benyon's having struck a note more serious than any that had hitherto souuded between them, looked at the sparse furniture, draped in white overalls, at the scagiiola floor, in which the great cluster of crystal pendants seemed to shine again.

"You are master of your ship. Can't you sail it as you like?" Kate Theory asked, with a smile.

"I am not master of anything. There is not a man in the world less free. I am a slave. I am a victim."

She looked at him with kind eyes; something in his voice suddenly made her put away all thought of the defensive airs that a girl, in certain situations, is expected to assume. She perceived that he wanted to make her understand something, and now her only wish was to help him to say it. "You are not happy," she murmured, simply, her voice dying away in a kind of wonderment at this reality.

The gentle touch of the words—it was as if her hand had stroked his cheek—seemed to him the sweetest thing he had ever known. "No, I am not happy, because I am not free. If I were—if I were, I would give up my ship. I would give up everything, to follow you. I can't explain; that is part of the hardness of it. I only want you to know it,—that if certain things were different, if everything was different, I might tell you that I believe I should have a right to speak to you. Perhaps some day it will change; but probably then it will be too late. Meanwhile, I have no right of any kind. I don't want to trouble you, and I don't ask of you—anything! It is only to have spoken just once. I don't make you understand, of course. I am afraid I seem to you rather a brute,—perhaps even a humbug. Don't think of it now,—don't try to understand. But some day, in the future, remember what I have said to you, and how we stood here, in this strange old place, alone! Perhaps it will give you a little pleasure."

Kate Theory began by listening to him with visible eagerness; but in a moment she turned away her eyes. "I am very sorry for you," she said, gravely.

"Then you do understand enough?"

"I shall think of what you have said, in the future."

Benyon's lips formed the beginning of a word of tenderness, which he instantly suppressed; and in a different tone, with a bitter smile and a sad shake of the head, raising his arms a moment and letting them fall, he said: "It won't hurt any one, your remembering this!"

"I don't know whom you mean." And the girl, abruptly, began to walk to the end of the room. He made no attempt to tell her whom he meant, and they proceeded together in silence till they overtook their companions.

There were several pictures in the neighboring room, and Percival Theory and his wife had stopped to look at one of them, of which the cicerone announced the title and the authorship as Benyon came up. It was a modern portrait of a Bourbon princess, a woman young, fair, handsome, covered with jewels. Mrs. Percival appeared to be more struck with it than with anything the palace had yet offered to her sight, while her sister-in-law walked to the window, which the custodian had opened, to look out into the garden. Benyon noticed this; he was conscious that he had given the girl something to reflect upon, and his ears burned a little as he stood beside Mrs. Percival and looked up, mechanically, at the royal lady. He already repented a little of what he had said, for, after all, what was the use? And he hoped the others wouldn't observe that he had been making love.

"Gracious, Percival! Do you see who she looks like?" Mrs. Theory said to her husband.

"She looks like a woman who has run up a big bill at Tiffany's," this gentleman answered.

"She looks like my sister-in-law; the eyes, the mouth, the way the hair's done,—the whole thing."

"Which do you mean? You have got about a dozen."

"Why, Georgina, of course,—Georgina Roy. She's awfully like."

"Do you call *her* your sister-in-law?" Percival Theory asked. "You must want very much to claim her."

"Well, she's handsome enough. You have got to invent some new name, then. Captain Benyon, what do you call your brother-in-law's second wife?" Mrs. Percival continued, turning to her neighbor, who still stood staring at the portrait. At first he had looked without seeing; then sight, and hearing as well, became quick. They were suddenly peopled with thrilling recognitions.

The Bourbon princess—the eyes, the mouth, the way the hair was done; these things took on an identity, and the gaze of the painted face seemed to fasten itself to his own. But who in the world was Georgina Roy, and what was this talk about sisters-in-law? He turned to the little lady at his side a countenance unexpectedly puzzled by the problem she had airily presented to him.

"Your brother-in-law's second wife? That's rather complicated."

"Well, of course, he need n't have married again?" said Mrs. Percival, with a small sigh.

"Whom did he marry?" asked Benyon, staring.

Percival Theory had turned away. "Oh, if you are going into her relationships!" he murmured, and joined his sister at the brilliant window, through which, from the distance, the many-voiced uproar of Naples came in.

"He married first my sister Dora, and she died five years ago. Then he married *her*," and Mrs. Percival nodded at the princess.

Benyon's eyes went back to the portrait; he could see what she meant—it stared out at him. "Her? Georgina?"

"Georgina Gressie. Gracious, do you know her?"

It was very distinct—that answer of Mrs. Percival's, and the question that followed it as well. But he had the resource of the picture; he could look at it, seem to take it very seriously, though it danced up and down before him. He felt that he was turning red, then he felt that he was turning pale. "The brazen impudence!" That was the way he could speak to himself now of the woman he had once loved, and whom he afterwards hated, till this had died out, too. Then the wonder of it was lost in the quickly growing sense that it would make a difference for him,—a great difference. Exactly what, he didn't see yet; only a difference that swelled and swelled as he thought of it, and caught up, in its expansion, the girl who stood behind him so quietly, looking into the Italian garden.

The custodian drew Mrs. Percival away to show her another princess, before Benyon answered her last inquiry. This gave him time to recover from his first impulse, which had been to answer it with a negative; he saw in a moment that an admission of his acquaintance with Mrs. Roy (Mrs. Roy!—it was prodigious!) was necessarily helping him to learn more. Besides, it needn't be compromising. Very likely Mrs. Percival would hear one day that he had once wanted to marry her. So, when he joined his companions a minute later he remarked that he had known Miss Gressie years before, and had even admired her considerably, but had lost sight of her entirely in later days. She had been a great beauty, and it was a wonder that she had not married earlier. Five years ago, was it? No, it was only two. He had been going to say that in so long a time it would have been singular he should not have heard of it. He had been away from New York for ages; but one always heard of marriages and deaths. This was a proof, though two years was rather long. He led Mrs. Percival insidiously into a further room, in advance of the others, to whom the cicerone returned. She was delighted to talk about her "connections," and she supplied him with every detail He could trust himself now; his self-possession was complete, or, so far as it was wanting, the fault was that of a sudden gayety which he could not, on the spot, have accounted for. Of course it was not very flattering to them—Mrs. Percivals own people—that poor Dora's husband should have consoled himself; but men always did it (talk of widows!) and he had chosen a girl who was—well, very fine-looking, and the sort of successor to Dora that they needn't be ashamed of. She had been awfully admired, and no one had understood why she had waited so long to marry. She had had some affair as a girl,—an engagement to an officer in the army,—and the man had jilted her, or they had quarrelled, or something or other. She was almost an old maid,—well, she was thirty, or very nearly,—but she had done something good now. She was handsomer than ever, and tremendously stylish. William Roy had one of the biggest incomes in the city, and he was quite affectionate. He had been intensely fond of Dora—he often spoke of her still, at least to her own relations; and her portrait, the last time Mrs. Percival was in his house (it was at a party, after his marriage to Miss Gressie), was still in the front parlor.. Perhaps by this time he had had it moved to the back; but she was sure he would keep it somewhere, anyway.

Poor Dora had had no children; but Georgina was making that all right,—
she had a beautiful boy. Mrs. Percival had what she would have called quite
a pleasant chat with Captain Benyon about Mrs. Roy. Perhaps *he* was the
officer—she never thought of that? He was sure he had never jilted her? And
he had never quarrelled with a lady? Well, he must be different from most
men.

He certainly had the air of being so, before he parted that afternoon
with Kate Theory. This young lady, at least, was free to think him wanting
in that consistency which is supposed to be a distinctively masculine virtue.
An hour before, he had taken an eternal farewell of her, and now he was
alluding to future meetings, to future visits, proposing that, with her sister-
in-law, she should appoint an early day for coming to see the "Louisiana."
She had supposed she understood him, but it would appear now that she
had not understood him at all. His manner had changed, too. More and
more off his guard, Raymond Benyon was not aware how much more hopeful
an expression it gave him, his irresistible sense that somehow or other this
extraordinary proceeding of his wife's would set him free. Kate Theory felt
rather weary and mystified,—all the more for knowing that henceforth
Captain Benyon's variations would be the most important thing in life for
her.

This officer, on his ship in the bay, lingered very late on deck that
night,—lingered there, indeed, under the warm southern sky, in which the
stars glittered with a hot, red light, until the early dawn began to show. He
smoked cigar after cigar, he walked up and down by the hour, he was agitated
by a thousand reflections, he repeated to himself that it made a difference,—
an immense difference; but the pink light had deepened in the east before
he had discovered in what the diversity consisted. By that time he saw it
clearly,—it consisted in Georgina's being in his power now, in place of his
being in hers. He laughed as he sat there alone in the darkness at the thought
of what she had done. It had occurred to him more than once that she would
do it,—he believed her capable of anything; but the accomplished fact had a
freshness of comicality. He thought of Mr. William Roy, of his big income,
of his being "quite affectionate," of his blooming son and heir, of his having

found such a worthy successor to poor Mrs. Dora. He wondered whether Georgina had happened to mention to him that she had a husband living, but was strongly of the belief that she had not. Why should she, after all? She had neglected to mention it to so many others. He had thought he knew her, in so many years,—that he had nothing more to learn about her; but this ripe stroke revived his sense of her audacity. Of course it was what she had been waiting for, and if she had not done it sooner it was because she had hoped he would be lost at sea in one of his long cruises and relieve her of the necessity of a crime. How she must hate him to-day for not having been lost, for being alive, for continuing to put her in the wrong! Much as she hated him, however, his own loathing was at least a match for hers. She had done him the foulest of wrongs,—she had ravaged his life. That he should ever detest in this degree a woman whom he had once loved as he loved her, he would not have thought possible in his innocent younger years. But he would not have thought it possible then that a woman should be such a cold-blooded devil as she had been. His love had perished in his rage,—his blinding, impotent rage at finding that he had been duped, and measuring his impotence. When he learned, years before, from Mrs. Portico, what she had done with her baby, of whose entrance into life she herself had given him no intimation, he felt that he was face to face with a full revelation of her nature. Before that it had puzzled him; it had amazed him; his relations with her were bewildering, stupefying. But when, after obtaining, with difficulty and delay, a leave of absence from Government, and betaking himself to Italy to look for the child and assume possession of it, he had encountered absolute failure and defeat,—then the case presented itself to him more simply. He perceived that he had mated himself with a creature who just happened to be a monster, a human exception altogether. That was what he could n't pardon—her conduct about the child; never, never, never! To him she might have done what she chose,—dropped him, pushed him out into eternal cold, with his hands fast tied,—and he would have accepted it, excused her almost, admitted that it had been his business to mind better what he was about. But she had tortured him through the poor little irrecoverable son whom he had never seen, through the heart and the vitals that she had not herself, and that he had to have, poor wretch, for both of them!

63

All his efforts for years had been to forget these horrible months, and he had cut himself off from them so that they seemed at times to belong to the life of another person. But to-night he lived them over again; he retraced the different gradations of darkness through which he had passed, from the moment, so soon after his extraordinary marriage, when it came over him that she already repented, and meant, if possible, to elude all her obligations. This was the moment when he saw why she had reserved herself—in the strange vow she extracted from him—an open door for retreat; the moment, too, when her having had such an inspiration (in the midst of her momentary good faith, if good faith it had ever been) struck him as a proof of her essential depravity. What he had tried to forget came back to him: the child that was not his child produced for him when he fell upon that squalid nest of peasants in the Genoese country; and then the confessions, retractations, contradictions, lies, terrors, threats, and general bottomless, baffling baseness of every one in the place. The child was gone; that had been the only definite thing. The woman who had taken it to nurse had a dozen different stories,—her husband had as many,—and every one in the village had a hundred more. Georgina had been sending money,—she had managed, apparently, to send a good deal,—and the whole country seemed to have been living on it and making merry. At one moment the baby had died and received a most expensive burial; at another he had been intrusted (for more healthy air, Santissima Madonna!) to the woman's cousin in another village. According to a version, which for a day or two Benyon had inclined to think the least false, he had been taken by the cousin (for his beauty's sake) to Genoa (when she went for the first time in her life to the town to see her daughter in service there), and had been confided for a few hours to a third woman, who was to keep him while the cousin walked about the streets, but who, having no child of her own, took such a fancy to him that she refused to give him up, and a few days later left the place (she was a Pisana) never to be heard of more. The cousin had forgotten her name,—it had happened six months before. Benyon spent a year looking up and down Italy for his child, and inspecting hundreds of swaddled infants, impenetrable candidates for recognition. Of course he could only get further and further from real knowledge, and his search was arrested by the conviction that it was making him mad. He set his teeth and made up his mind (or tried to) that the baby had died in the hands of its nurse. This was, after all, much the likeliest supposition, and the woman had maintained it, in the hope of being rewarded for her candor, quite as often as she had asseverated that it was still, somewhere, alive, in the hope of being remunerated for her good news. It may be imagined with what sentiments toward his wife Benyon had emerged from this episode. To-night his memory went further back,—back to the beginning and to the days when he had had to ask himself, with all the crudity of his first surprise, what in the name of wantonness she had wished to do with him. The answer to this speculation was so old,—it had dropped so ont of the line of recurrence,— that it was now almost new again. Moreover, it was only approximate, for, as I have already said, he could comprehend such conduct as little at the end as at the beginning. She had found herself on a slope which her nature forced her to descend to the bottom. She did him the honor of wishing to enjoy his society, and she did herself the honor of thinking that their intimacy— however brief—must have a certain consecration. She felt that, with him, after his promise (he would have made any promise to lead her on), she was secure,—secure as she had proved to be, secure as she must think herself now. That security had helped her to ask herself, after the first flush of passion was over, and her native, her twice-inherited worldliness had bad time to open its eyes again, why she should keep faith with a man whose deficiencies (as a husband before the world—another affair) had been so scientifically exposed to her by her parents. So she had simply determined not to keep faith; and her determination, at least, she did keep.

By the time Benyon turned in he had satisfied himself, as I say, that Georgina was now in his power; and this seemed to him such an improvement in his situation that he allowed himself (for the next ten days) a license which made Kate Theory almost as happy as it made her sister, though she pretended to understand it far less. Mildred sank to her rest, or rose to fuller comprehensions, within the year, in the Isle of Wight, and Captain Benyon, who had never written so many letters as since they left Naples, sailed westward about the same time as the sweet survivor. For the "Louisiana" at last was ordered home.

VI.

Certainly, I will see you if you come, and you may appoint any day or hour you like. I should have seen you with pleasure any time these last years. Why should we not be friends, as we used to be? Perhaps we shall be yet. I say "perhaps" only, on purpose,—because your note is rather vague about your state of mind. Don't come with any idea about making me nervous or uncomfortable. I am not nervous by nature, thank Heaven, and I won't—I positively won't (do you hear, dear Captain Benyon?)—be uncomfortable. I have been so (it served me right) for years and years; but I am very happy now. To remain so is the very definite intention of, yours ever,

Georgina Roy.

This was the answer Benyon received to a short letter that he despatched to Mrs. Roy after his return to America. It was not till he had been there some weeks that he wrote to her. He had been occupied in various ways: he had had to look after his ship; he had had to report at Washington; he had spent a fortnight with his mother at Portsmouth, N. H.; and he had paid a visit to Kate Theory in Boston. She herself was paying visits, she was staying with various relatives and friends. She had more color—it was very delicately rosy—than she had had of old, in spite of her black dress; and the effect of looking at him seemed to him to make her eyes grow still prettier. Though sisterless now, she was not without duties, and Benyon could easily see that life would press hard on her unless some one should interfere. Every one regarded her as just the person to do certain things. Every one thought she could do everything, because she had nothing else to do. She used to read to the blind, and, more onerously, to the deaf. She looked after other people's children while the parents attended anti-slavery conventions.

She was coming to New York later to spend a week at her brother's, but beyond this she didn't know what she should do. Benyon felt it to be awkward that he should not be able, just now, to tell her; and this had much to do with his coming to the point, for he accused himself of having rather hung fire. Coming to the point, for Benyon, meant writing a note to Mrs. Roy (as he must call her), in which he asked whether she would see him if he should present himself. The missive was short; it contained, in addition to what I have noted, little more than the remark that he had something of importance to say to her. Her reply, which we have just read, was prompt. Benyon designated an hour, and the next day rang the doorbell of her big modern house, whose polished windows seemed to shine defiance at him.

As he stood on the steps, looking up and down the straight vista of the Fifth Avenue, he perceived that he was trembling a little, that *he* was nervous, if she was not. He was ashamed of his agitation, and he addressed himself a very stern reprimand. Afterwards he saw that what had made him nervous was not any doubt of the goodness of his cause, but his revived sense (as he drew near her) of his wife's hardness,—her capacity for insolence. He might only break himself against that, and the prospect made him feel helpless. She kept him waiting for a long time after he had been introduced; and as he walked up and down her drawing-room, an immense, florid, expensive apartment, covered with blue satin, gilding, mirrors and bad frescos, it came over him as a certainty that her delay was calculated. She wished to annoy him, to weary him; she was as ungenerous as she was unscrupulous. It never occurred to him that in spite of the bold words of her note, she, too, might be in a tremor, and if any one in their secret had suggested that she was afraid to meet him, he would have laughed at this idea. This was of bad omen for the success of his errand; for it showed that he recognized the ground of her presumption,—his having the superstition of old promises. By the time she appeared, he was flushed,—very angry. She closed the door behind her, and stood there looking at him, with the width of the room between them.

The first emotion her presence excited was a quick sense of the strange fact that, after all these years of loneliness, such a magnificent person should be his wife. For she was magnificent, in the maturity of her beauty, her head erect, her complexion splendid, her auburn tresses undimmed, a certain plenitude in her very glance. He saw in a moment that she wished to seem to him beautiful, she had endeavored to dress herself to the best effect. Perhaps, after all, it was only for this she had delayed; she wished to give herself every possible touch. For some moments they said nothing; they had not stood face to face for nearly ten years, and they met now as adversaries. No two persons could possibly be more interested in taking each other's measure. It scarcely belonged to Georgina, however, to have too much the air of timidity; and after a moment, satisfied, apparently, that she was not to receive a broadside, she advanced, slowly rubbing her jewelled hands and smiling. He wondered why she should smile, what thought was in her mind. His impressions followed each other with extraordinary quickness of pulse, and now he saw, in addition to what he had already perceived, that she was waiting to take her cue,—she had determined on no definite line. There was nothing definite about her but her courage; the rest would depend upon him. As for her courage, it seemed to glow in the beauty which grew greater as she came nearer, with her eyes on his and her fixed smile; to be expressed in the very perfume that accompanied her steps. By this time he had got still a further impression, and it was the strangest of all. She was ready for anything, she was capable of anything, she wished to surprise him with her beauty, to remind him that it belonged, after all, at the bottom of everything, to him. She was ready to bribe him, if bribing should be necessary. She had carried on an intrigue before she was twenty; it would be more, rather than less, easy for her, now that she was thirty. All this and more was in her cold, living eyes, as in the prolonged silence they engaged themselves with his; but I must not dwell upon it, for reasons extraneous to the remarkable fact She was a truly amazing creature.

"Raymond!" she said, in a low voice, a voice which might represent either a vague greeting or an appeal.

He took no heed of the exclamation, but asked her why she had deliberately kept him waiting,—as if she had not made a fool enough of him already. She could n't suppose it was for his pleasure he had come into the house.

She hesitated a moment,—still with her smile. "I must tell you I have a son,—the dearest little boy. His nurse happened to be engaged for the moment, and I had to watch him. I am more devoted to him than you might suppose."

He fell back from her a few steps. "I wonder if you are insane," he murmured.

"To allude to my child? Why do you ask me such questions then? I tell you the simple truth. I take every care of this one. I am older and wiser. The other one was a complete mistake; he had no right to exist."

"Why didn't you kill him then with your own hands, instead of that torture?"

"Why did n't I kill myself? That question would be more to the point You are looking wonderfully well," she broke off in another tone; "had n't we better sit down?"

"I did n't come here for the advantage of conversation," Benyon answered. And he was going on, but she interrupted him—

"You came to say something dreadful, very likely; though I hoped you would see it was better not But just tell me this before you begin. Are you successful, are you happy? It has been so provoking, not knowing more about you."

There was something in the manner in which this was said that caused him to break into a loud laugh; whereupon she added,—

"Your laugh is just what it used to be. How it comes back to me! You *have* improved in appearance," she went on.

She had seated herself, though he remained standing; and she leaned back in a low, deep chair, looking up at him, with her arms folded. He stood near her and over her, as it were, dropping his baffled eyes on her, with his hand resting on the corner of the chimney-piece. "Has it never occurred to you that I may deem myself absolved from the promise made you before I married you?"

"Very often, of course. But I have instantly dismissed the idea. How can you be 'absolved'? One promises, or one doesn't. I attach no meaning to that, and neither do you." And she glanced down to the front of her dress.

Benyon listened, but he went on as if he had not heard her. "What I came to say to you is this: that I should like your consent to my bringing a suit for divorce against you."

"A suit for divorce? I never thought of that."

"So that I may marry another woman. I can easily obtain a divorce on the ground of your desertion."

She stared a moment, then her smile solidified, as it were, and she looked grave; but he could see that her gravity, with her lifted eyebrows, was partly assumed. "Ah, you want to marry another woman!" she exclaimed, slowly, thoughtfully. He said nothing, and she went on: "Why don't you do as I have done?"

"Because I don't want my children to be—"

Before he could say the words she sprang up, checking him with a cry. "Don't say it; it is n't necessary! Of course I know what you mean; but they won't be if no one knows it."

"I should object to knowing it myself; it's enough for me to know it of yours."

"Of course I have been prepared for your saying that"

"I should hope so!" Benyon exclaimed. "You may be a bigamist if it suits you, but to me the idea is not attractive. I wish to marry—" and, hesitating a moment, with his slight stammer, he repeated, "I wish to marry—"

"Marry, then, and have done with it!" cried Mrs. Roy.

He could already see that he should be able to extract no consent from her; he felt rather sick. "It's extraordinary to me that you should n't be more afraid of being found out," he said after a moment's reflection. "There are two or three possible accidents."

"How do you know how much afraid I am? I have thought of every accident, in dreadful nights. How do you know what my life is, or what it has been all these miserable years?"

"You look wasted and worn, certainly."

"Ah, don't compliment me!" Georgina exclaimed. "If I had never known you—if I had not been through all this—I believe I should have been handsome. When did you hear of my marriage? Where were you at the time?"

"At Naples, more than six months ago, by a mere chance."

"How strange that it should have taken you so long! Is the lady a Neapolitan? They don't mind what they do over there."

"I have no information to give you beyond what I just said," Benyon rejoined. "My life does n't in the least regard you."

"Ah, but it does from the moment I refuse to let you divorce me."

"You refuse?" Benyon said softly.

"Don't look at me that way! You have n't advanced so rapidly as I used to think you would; you haven't distinguished yourself so much," she went on, irrelevantly.

"I shall be promoted commodore one of these days," Benyon answered. "You don't know much about it, for my advancement has already been very exceptionally rapid." He blushed as soon as the words were out of his mouth. She gave a light laugh on seeing it; but he took up his hat and added: "Think over a day or two what I have proposed to you. Think of the temper in which I ask it."

"The temper?" she stared. "Pray, what have you to do with temper?" And as he made no reply, smoothing his hat with his glove, she went on: "Years ago, as much as you please I you had a good right, I don't deny, and you raved, in your letters, to your heart's content That's why I would n't see you; I did n't wish to take it full in the face. But that's all over now, time is a healer, you have cooled off, and by your own admission you have consoled yourself. Why do you talk to me about temper! What in the world have I done to you, but let you alone?"

"What do you call this business?" Benyon asked, with his eye flashing all over the room.

71

"Ah, excuse me, that doesn't touch you,—it's my affair. I leave you your liberty, and I can live as I like. If I choose to live in this way, it may be queer (I admit it is, awfully), but you have nothing to say to it. If I am willing to take the risk, you may be. If I am willing to play such an infernal trick upon a confiding gentleman (I will put it as strongly as you possibly could), I don't see what you have to say to it except that you are tremendously glad such a woman as that is n't known to be your wife!" She had been cool and deliberate up to this time; but with these words her latent agitation broke out "Do you think I have been happy? Do you think I have enjoyed existence? Do you see me freezing up into a stark old maid?"

"I wonder you stood out so long!" said Benyon.

"I wonder I did. They were bad years."

"I have no doubt they were!"

"You could do as you pleased," Georgina went on. "You roamed about the world; you formed charming relations. I am delighted to hear it from your own lips. Think of my going back to my father's house—that family vault—and living there, year after year, as Miss Gressie! If you remember my father and mother—they are round in Twelfth Street, just the same—you must admit that I paid for my folly!"

"I have never understood you; I don't understand you now," said Benyon.

She looked at him a moment. "I adored you."

"I could damn you with a word!" he went on.

The moment he had spoken she grasped his arm and held up her other hand, as if she were listening to a sound outside the room. She had evidently had an inspiration, and she carried it into instant effect She swept away to the door, flung it open, and passed into the hall, whence her voice came back to Benyon as she addressed a person who was apparently her husband. She had heard him enter the house at his habitual hour, after his long morning at business; the closing of the door of the vestibule had struck her ear. The parlor was on a level with the hall, and she greeted him without impediment.

She asked him to come in and be introduced to Captain Benyon, and he responded with due solemnity. She returned in advance of him, her eyes fixed upon Benyon and lighted with defiance, her whole face saying to him, vividly: "Here is your opportunity; I give it to you with my own hands. Break your promise and betray me if you dare! You say you can damn me with a word: speak the word and let us see!"

Benyon's heart beat faster, as he felt that it was indeed a chance; but half his emotion came from the spectacle—magnificent in its way—of her unparalleled impudence. A sense of all that he had escaped in not having had to live with her rolled over him like a wave, while he looked strangely at Mr. Roy, to whom this privilege had been vouchsafed. He saw in a moment his successor had a constitution that would carry it. Mr. Roy suggested squareness and solidity; he was a broadbased, comfortable, polished man, with a surface in which the rank tendrils of irritation would not easily obtain a foothold. He had a broad, blank face, a capacious mouth, and a small, light eye, to which, as he entered, he was engaged in adjusting a double gold-rimmed glass. He approached Benyon with a prudent, civil, punctual air, as if he habitually met a good many gentlemen in the course of business, and though, naturally, this was not that sort of occasion he was not a man to waste time in preliminaries. Benyon had immediately the impression of having seen him—or his equivalent—a thousand times before. He was middle-aged, fresh-colored, whiskered, prosperous, indefinite. Georgina introduced them to each other. She spoke of Benyon as an old friend whom she had known long before she had known Mr. Roy, who had been very kind to her years ago, when she was a girl.

"He's in the navy. He has just come back from a long cruise."

Mr. Hoy shook hands,—Benyon gave him his before he knew it,—said he was very happy, smiled, looked at Benyon from head to foot, then at Georgina, then round the room, then back at Benyon again,—at Benyon, who stood there, without sound or movement, with a dilated eye, and a pulse quickened to a degree of which Mr. Roy could have little idea. Georgina made some remark about their sitting down, but William Roy replied that he had n't time for that,—if Captain Benyon would excuse him. He should have to go straight into the library, and write a note to send back to his office, where, as he just remembered, he had neglected to give, in leaving the place, an important direction.

"You can wait a moment, surely," Georgina said. "Captain Benyon wants so much to see you."

"Oh, yes, my dear; I can wait a minute, and I can come back."

Benyon saw, accordingly, that he was waiting, and that Georgina was waiting too. Each was waiting for him to say something, though they were waiting for different things. Mr. Roy put his hands behind him, balanced himself on his toes, hoped that Captain Benyon had enjoyed his cruise,—though he should n't care much for the navy himself,—and evidently wondered at the stolidity of his wife's visitor. Benyon knew he was speaking, for he indulged in two or three more observations, after which he stopped. But his meaning was not present to our hero. This personage was conscious of only one thing, of his own momentary power,—of everything that hung on his lips; all the rest swam before him; there was vagueness in his ears and eyes. Mr. Roy stopped, as I say, and there was a pause, which seemed to Benyon of tremendous length. He knew, while it lasted, that Georgina was as conscious as himself that he felt his opportunity, that he held it there in his hand, weighing it noiselessly in the palm, and that she braved and scorned, or, rather, that she enjoyed, the danger. He asked himself whether he should be able to speak if he were to try, and then he knew that he should not, that the words would stick in his throat, that he should make sounds that would dishonor his cause. There was no real choice or decision, then, on Benyon's part; his silence was after all the same old silence, the fruit of other hours and places, the stillness to which Georgina listened, while he felt her eager eyes fairly eat into his face, so that his cheeks burned with the touch of them. The moments stood before him in their turn; each one was distinct. "Ah, well," said Mr. Roy, "perhaps I interrupt,—I 'll just dash off my note" Benyon knew that he was rather bewildered, that he was making a pretext, that he was leaving the room; knew presently that Georgina again stood before him alone.

"You are exactly the man I thought you!" she announced, as joyously as if she had won a bet.

"You are the most horrible woman I can imagine. Good God! if I *had* had to live with you!" That is what he said to her in answer.

Even at this she never flushed; she continued to smile in triumph. "He adores me—but what's that to you? Of course you have all the future," she went on; "but I know you as if I had made you!"

Benyon reflected a moment "If he adores you, you are all right. If our divorce is pronounced, you will be free, and then he can marry you properly, which he would like ever so much better."

"It's too touching to hear you reason about it. Fancy me telling such a hideous story—about myself—me—*me!*" And she touched her breasts with her white fingers.

Benyon gave her a look that was charged with all the sickness of his helpless rage. "You—*you!*" he repeated, as he turned away from her and passed through the door which Mr. Roy had left open.

She followed him into the hall, she was close behind him; he moved before her as she pressed. "There was one more reason," she said. "I would n't be forbidden. It was my hideous pride. That's what prevents me now."

"I don't care what it is," Benyon answered, wearily, with his hand on the knob of the door.

She laid hers on his shoulder; he stood there an instant feeling it, wishing that her loathsome touch gave him the right to strike her to the earth,—to strike her so that she should never rise again.

"How clever you are, and intelligent always,—as you used to be; to feel so perfectly and know so well, without more scenes, that it's hopeless—my ever consenting! If I have, with you, the shame of having made you promise, let me at least have the profit!"

His back had been turned to her, but at this he glanced round. "To hear you talk of shame—!"

"You don't know what I have gone through; but, of course, I don't ask any pity from you. Only I should like to say something kind to you before we part I admire you, esteem you: I don't many people! Who will ever tell her, if you don't? How will she ever know, then? She will be as safe as I am. You know what that is," said Georgina, smiling.

He had opened the door while she spoke, apparently not heeding her, thinking only of getting away from her forever. In reality he heard every word she said, and felt to his marrow the lowered, suggestive tone in which she made him that last recommendation. Outside, on the steps—she stood there in the doorway—he gave her his last look. "I only hope you will die. I shall pray for that!" And he descended into the street and took his way.

It was after this that his real temptation came. Not the temptation to return betrayal for betrayal; that passed away even in a few days, for he simply knew that he couldn't break his promise, that it imposed itself on him as stubbornly as the color of his eyes or the stammer of his lips; it had gone forth into the world to live for itself, and was far beyond his reach or his authority. But the temptation to go through the form of a marriage with Kate Theory, to let her suppose that he was as free as herself, and that their children, if they should have any, would, before the law, have a right to exist,—this attractive idea held him fast for many weeks, and caused him to pass some haggard nights and days. It was perfectly possible she might learn his secret, and that, as no one could either suspect it or have an interest in bringing it to light, they both might live and die in security and honor. This vision fascinated him; it was, I say, a real temptation. He thought of other solutions,—of telling her that he was married (without telling her to whom), and inducing her to overlook such an accident, and content herself with a ceremony in which the world would see no flaw. But after all the contortions of his spirit it remained as clear to him as before that dishonor was in everything but renunciation. So, at last, he renounced. He took two steps which attested ths act to himself. He addressed an urgent request to the Secretary of the Navy that he might, with as little delay as possible, be despatched on another long voyage; and he returned to Boston to tell Kate Theory that they must wait. He could explain so little that, say what he would, he was aware that he could not make his conduct seem natural, and he saw that the girl only trusted him,—that she never understood. She trusted without understanding, and she agreed to wait. When the writer of these pages last heard of the pair they were waiting still.

THE PATH OF DUTY

I am glad I said to you the other night at Doubleton, inquiring—too inquiring—compatriot, that I wouldn't undertake to tell you the story (about Ambrose Tester), but would write it out for you; inasmuch as, thinking it over since I came back to town, I see that it may really be made interesting. It *is* a story, with a regular development, and for telling it I have the advantage that I happened to know about it from the first, and was more or less in the confidence of every one concerned. Then it will amuse me to write it, and I shall do so as carefully and as cleverly as possible The first winter days in London are not madly gay, so that I have plenty of time; and if the fog is brown outside, the fire is red within. I like the quiet of this season; the glowing chimney-corner, in the midst of the December mirk, makes me think, as I sit by it, of all sorts of things. The idea that is almost always uppermost is the bigness and strangeness of this London world. Long as I have lived here,—the sixteenth anniversary of my marriage is only ten days off,—there is still a kind of novelty and excitement in it It is a great pull, as they say here, to have remained sensitive,—to have kept one's own point of view. I mean it's more entertaining,—it makes you see a thousand things (not that they are all very charming). But the pleasure of observation does not in the least depend on the beauty of what one observes. You see innumerable little dramas; in fact, almost everything has acts and scenes, like a comedy. Very often it is a comedy with tears. There have been a good many of them, I am afraid, in the case I am speaking of. It is because this history of Sir Ambrose Tester and Lady Vandeleur struck me, when you asked me about the relations of the parties, as having that kind of progression, that when I was on the point of responding, I checked myself, thinking it a pity to tell you a little when I might tell you all. I scarcely know what made you ask, inasmuch as I had said nothing to excite your curiosity. Whatever you suspected, you suspected on your own hook, as they say. You had simply noticed the pair together that evening at Doubleton. If you suspected anything in particular, it is a proof that you are rather sharp, because they are very careful about the way they behave in public. At least they think they are. The result, perhaps, doesn't necessarily follow. If I have been in their confidence you may say that I make a strange use of my privilege in serving them up to feed the prejudices of an opinionated American. You think English society very wicked, and my little story will probably not correct the impression. Though, after all, I don't see why it should minister to it; for what I said to you (it was all I did say) remains the truth. They are treading together the path of duty. You would be quite right about its being base in me to betray them. It is very true that they have ceased to confide in me; even Joscelind has said nothing to me for more than a year. That is doubtless a sign that the situation is more serious than before, all round,—too serious to be talked about. It is also true that you are remarkably discreet, and that even if you were not it would not make much difference, inasmuch as if you were to repeat my revelations in America, no one would know whom you were talking about. But all the same, I should be base; and, therefore, after I have written out my reminiscences for your delectation, I shall simply keep them for my own. You must content yourself with the explanation I have already given you of Sir Ambrose Tester and Lady Vandeleur: they are following—hand in hand, as it were—the path of duty. This will not prevent me from telling everything; on the contrary, don't you see?

I.

His brilliant prospects dated from the death of his brother, who had no children, had indeed steadily refused to marry. When I say brilliant prospects, I mean the vision of the baronetcy, one of the oldest in England, of a charming seventeenth-century house, with its park, in Dorsetshire, and a property worth some twenty thousand a year. Such a collection of items is still dazzling to me, even after what you would call, I suppose, a familiarity with British grandeur. My husband is n't a baronet (or we probably should n't be in London in December), and he is far, alas, from having twenty thousand a year. The full enjoyment of these luxuries, on Ambrose Tester's part, was dependent naturally, on the death of his father, who was still very much to the fore at the time I first knew the young man. The proof of it is the way he kept nagging at his sons, as the younger used to say, on the question of taking a wife. The nagging had been of no avail, as I have mentioned, with regard to Francis, the elder, whose affections were centred (his brother himself told me) on the winecup and the faro-table. He was not an exemplary or edifying character, and as the heir to an honorable name and a fine estate was very unsatisfactory indeed. It had been possible in those days to put him into the army, but it was not possible to keep him there; and he was still a very young man when it became plain that any parental dream of a "career" for Frank Tester was exceedingly vain. Old Sir Edmund had thought matrimony would perhaps correct him, but a sterner process than this was needed, and it came to him one day at Monaco—he was most of the time abroad—after an illness so short that none of the family arrived in time. He was reformed altogether, he was utterly abolished.

The second son, stepping into his shoes, was such an improvement that it was impossible there should be much simulation of mourning. You have seen him, you know what he is; there is very little mystery about him. As I am not going to show this composition to you, there is no harm in my writing here that he is—or at any rate he was—a remarkably attractive man. I don't say this because he made love to me, but precisely because he did n't. He was always in love with some one else,—generally with Lady Vandeleur. You may say that in England that usually does n't prevent; but Mr. Tester, though he had almost no intermissions, did n't, as a general thing, have duplicates. He was not provided with a second loved object, "under-studying," as they say, the part. It was his practice to keep me accurately informed of the state of his affections,—a matter about which he was never in the least vague. When he was in love he knew it and rejoiced in it, and when by a miracle he was not he greatly regretted it. He expatiated to me on the charms of other persons, and this interested me much more than if he had attempted to direct the conversation to my own, as regards which I had no illusions. He has told me some singular things, and I think I may say that for a considerable period my most valued knowledge of English society was extracted from this genial youth. I suppose he usually found me a woman of good counsel, for certain it is that he has appealed to me for the light of wisdom in very extraordinary predicaments. In his earlier years he was perpetually in hot water; he tumbled into scrapes as children tumble into puddles. He invited them, he invented them; and when he came to tell you how his trouble had come about (and he always told the whole truth), it was difficult to believe that a man should have been so idiotic.

And yet he was not an idiot; he was supposed to be very clever, and certainly is very quick and amusing. He was only reckless, and extraordinarily natural, as natural as if he had been an Irishman. In fact, of all the Englishmen that I have known he is the most Irish in temperament (though he has got over it comparatively of late). I used to tell him that it was a great inconvenience that he didn't speak with a brogue, because then we should be forewarned, and know with whom we were dealing. He replied that, by analogy, if he were Irish enough to have a brogue he would probably be English, which seemed to me an answer wonderfully in character. Like most young Britons of his class he went to America, to see the great country, before he was twenty, and he took a letter to my father, who had occasion, *à propos* of some pickle of course, to render him a considerable service. This led to his coming to see me—I had already been living here three or four years—on his return; and that, in the course of time, led to our becoming fast friends, without, as I tell you, the smallest philandering on either side. But I must n't protest too much;

I shall excite your suspicion. "If he has made love to so many women, why should n't he have made love to you?"—some inquiry of that sort you will be likely to make. I have answered it already, "Simply on account of those very engagements." He could n't make love to every one, and with me it would n't have done him the least good. It was a more amiable weakness than his brother's, and he has always behaved very well. How well he behaved on a very important occasion is precisely the subject of my story.

He was supposed to have embraced the diplomatic career; had been secretary of legation at some German capital; but after his brother's death he came home and looked out for a seat in Parliament. He found it with no great trouble and has kept it ever since. No one would have the heart to turn him out, he is so good-looking. It's a great thing to be represented by one of the handsomest men in England, it creates such a favorable association of ideas. Any one would be amazed to discover that the borough he sits for, and the name of which I am always forgetting, is not a very pretty place. I have never seen it, and have no idea that it is n't, and I am sure he will survive every revolution. The people must feel that if they should n't keep him some monster would be returned. You remember his appearance,—how tall, and fair, and strong he is, and always laughing, yet without looking silly. He is exactly the young man girls in America figure to themselves—in the place of the hero—when they read English novels, and wish to imagine something very aristocratic and Saxon. A "bright Bostonian" who met him once at my house, exclaimed as soon as he had gone out of the room, "At last, at last, I behold it, the mustache of Roland Tremayne!"

"Of Roland Tremayne!"

"Don't you remember in *A Lawless Love*, how often it's mentioned, and how glorious and golden it was? Well, I have never seen it till now, but now I *have* seen it!"

If you had n't seen Ambrose Tester, the best description I could give of him would be to say that he looked like Roland Tremayne. I don't know whether that hero was a "strong Liberal," but this is what Sir Ambrose is supposed to be. (He succeeded his father two years ago, but I shall come to that.) He is not exactly what I should call thoughtful, but he is interested, or thinks he is, in a lot of things that I don't understand, and that one sees and skips in the newspapers,—volunteering, and redistribution, and sanitation, and the representation of minors—minorities—what is it? When I said just now that he is always laughing, I ought to have explained that I did n't mean when he is talking to Lady Vandeleur. She makes him serious, makes him almost solemn; by which I don't mean that she bores him. Far from it; but when he is in her company he is thoughtful; he pulls his golden mustache, and Roland Tremayne looks as if his vision were turned in, and he were meditating on her words. He does n't say much himself; it is she—she used to be so silent— who does the talking. She has plenty to say to him; she describes to him the charms that she discovers in the path of duty. He seldom speaks in the House, I believe, but when he does it's offhand, and amusing, and sensible, and every one likes it. He will never be a great statesman, but he will add to the softness of Dorsetshire, and remain, in short, a very gallant, pleasant, prosperous, typical English gentleman, with a name, a fortune, a perfect appearance, a devoted, bewildered little wife, a great many reminiscences, a great many friends (including Lady Vandeleur and myself), and, strange to say, with all these advantages, something that faintly resembles a conscience.

II.

Five years ago he told me his father insisted on his marrying,—would not hear of his putting it off any longer. Sir Edmund had been harping on this string ever since he came back from Germany, had made it both a general and a particular request, not only urging him to matrimony in the abstract, but pushing him into the arms of every young woman in the country. Ambrose had promised, procrastinated, temporized; but at last he was at the end of his evasions, and his poor father had taken the tone of supplication. "He thinks immensely of the name, of the place and all that, and he has got it into his head that if I don't marry before he dies, I won't marry after." So much I remember Ambrose Tester said to me. "It's a fixed idea; he has got it on the brain. He wants to see me married with his eyes, and he wants to take his grandson in his arms. Not without that will he be satisfied that the whole thing will go straight. He thinks he is nearing his end, but he isn't,—he will live to see a hundred, don't you think so?—and he has made me a solemn appeal to put an end to what he calls his suspense. He has an idea some one will get hold of me—some woman I can't marry. As if I were not old enough to take care of myself!"

"Perhaps he is afraid of me," I suggested, facetiously.

"No, it is n't you," said my visitor, betraying by his tone that it was some one, though he didn't say whom. "That's all rot, of course; one marries sooner or later, and I shall do like every one else. If I marry before I die, it's as good as if I marry before he dies, is n't it? I should be delighted to have the governor at my wedding, but it is n't necessary for the legality, is it?"

I asked him what he wished me to do, and how I could help him. He knew already my peculiar views, that I was trying to get husbands for all the girls of my acquaintance and to prevent the men from taking wives. The sight of an ummarried woman afflicted me, and yet when my male friends changed their state I took it as a personal offence. He let me know that so far as he was concerned I must prepare myself for this injury, for he had given his father his word that another twelvemonth should not see him a bachelor. The old man had given him *carte blanche*; he made no condition beyond exacting that the lady should have youth and health. Ambrose Tester, at any rate, had taken a vow and now he was going seriously to look about him. I said to him that what must be must be, and that there were plenty of charming girls about the land, among whom he could suit himself easily enough. There was no better match in England, I said, and he would only have to make his choice. That however is not what I thought, for my real reflections were summed up in the silent exclamation, "What a pity Lady Vandeleur isn't a widow!" I hadn't the smallest doubt that if she were he would marry her on the spot; and after he had gone I wondered considerably what *she* thought of this turn in his affairs. If it was disappointing to me, how little it must be to *her* taste! Sir Edmund had not been so much out of the way in fearing there might be obstacles to his son's taking the step he desired. Margaret Vandeleur was an obstacle. I knew it as well as if Mr. Tester had told me.

I don't mean there was anything in their relation he might not freely have alluded to, for Lady Vandeleur, in spite of her beauty and her tiresome husband, was not a woman who could be accused of an indiscretion. Her husband was a pedant about trifles,—the shape of his hatbrim, the *pose* of his coachman, and cared for nothing else; but she was as nearly a saint as one may be when one has rubbed shoulders for ten years with the best society in Europe. It is a characteristic of that society that even its saints are suspected, and I go too far in saying that little pinpricks were not administered, in considerable numbers to her reputation. But she did n't feel them, for still more than Ambrose Tester she was a person to whose happiness a good conscience was necessary. I should almost say that for her happiness it was sufficient, and, at any rate, it was only those who didn't know her that pretended to speak of her lightly. If one had the honor of her acquaintance one might have thought her rather shut up to her beauty and her grandeur, but one could n't but feel there was something in her composition that would keep her from vulgar aberrations. Her husband was such a feeble type that she must have felt doubly she had been put upon her honor. To deceive such a man as that was to make him more ridiculous than he was already, and from such a result a woman bearing his name may very well have shrunk. Perhaps it would have been worse for Lord Vandeleur, who had every pretension of his order and none of its amiability, if he had been a better, or at least, a cleverer man. When a woman behaves so well she is not obliged to be careful, and there is no need of consulting appearances when one is one's self an appearance. Lady Vandeleur accepted Ambrose Tester's attentions, and Heaven knows they were frequent; but she had such an air of perfect equilibrium that one could n't see her, in imagination, bend responsive. Incense was incense, but one saw her sitting quite serene among the fumes. That honor of her acquaintance of which I just now spoke it had been given me to enjoy; that is to say, I met her a dozen times in the season in a hot crowd, and we smiled sweetly and murmured a vague question or two, without hearing, or even trying to hear, each other's answer. If I knew that Ambrose Tester was perpetually in and out of her house and always arranging with her that they should go to the same places, I doubt whether she, on her side, knew how often he came to see me. I don't think he would have let her know, and am conscious, in saying this, that it indicated an advanced state of intimacy (with her, I mean).

I also doubt very much whether he asked her to look about, on his behalf, for a future Lady Tester. This request he was so good as to make of me; but I told him I would have nothing to do with the matter. If Joscelind is unhappy, I am thankful to say the responsibility is not mine. I have found English husbands for two or three American girls, but providing English wives is a different affair. I know the sort of men that will suit women, but one would have to be very clever to know the sort of women that will suit men. I told Ambrose Tester that he must look out for himself, but, in spite of his promise, I had very little belief that he would do anything of the sort. I thought it probable that the old baronet would pass away without seeing a new generation come in; though when I intimated as much to Mr. Tester, he made answer in substance (it was not quite so crudely said) that his father, old as he was, would hold on till his bidding was done, and if it should not be done, he would hold on out of spite. "Oh, he will tire me out;" that I remember Ambrose Tester did say. I had done him injustice, for six months later he told me he was engaged. It had all come about very suddenly. From one day to the other the right young woman had been found. I forget who had found her; some aunt or cousin, I think; it had not been the young man himself. But when she was found, he rose to the occasion; he took her up seriously, he approved of her thoroughly, and I am not sure that he didn't fall a little in love with her, ridiculous (excuse my London tone) as this accident may appear. He told me that his father was delighted, and I knew afterwards that he had good reason to be. It was not till some weeks later that I saw the girl; but meanwhile I had received the pleasantest impression of her, and this impression came—must have come—mainly from what her intended told me. That proves that he spoke with some positiveness, spoke as if he really believed he was doing a good thing. I had it on my tongue's end to ask him how Lady Vandeleur liked her, but I fortunately checked this vulgar inquiry. He liked her evidently, as I say; every one liked her, and when I knew her I liked her better even than the others. I like her to-day more than ever; it is fair you should know that, in reading this account of her situation. It doubtless colors my picture, gives a point to my sense of the strangeness of my little story.

Joscelind Bernardstone came of a military race, and had been brought up in camps,—by which I don't mean she was one of those objectionable young women who are known as garrison hacks. She was in the flower of her freshness, and had been kept in the tent, receiving, as an only daughter, the most "particular" education from the excellent Lady Emily (General Bernardstone married a daughter of Lord Clandufly), who looks like a pink-faced rabbit, and is (after Joscelind) one of the nicest women I know. When I met them in a country-house, a few weeks after the marriage was "arranged," as they say here, Joscelind won my affections by saying to me, with her timid directness (the speech made me feel sixty years old), that she must thank me for having been so kind to Mr. Tester. You saw her at Doubleton, and you will remember that though she has no regular beauty, many a prettier woman would be very glad to look like her. She is as fresh as a new-laid egg, as light as a feather, as strong as a mail-phaeton. She is perfectly mild, yet she is clever enough to be sharp if she would. I don't know that clever women are necessarily thought ill-natured, but it is usually taken for granted that amiable women are very limited. Lady Tester is a refutation of the theory, which must have been invented by a vixenish woman who was *not* clever. She has an adoration for her husband, which absorbs her without in the least making her silly, unless indeed it is silly to be modest, as in this brutal world I sometimes believe. Her modesty is so great that being unhappy has hitherto presented itself to her as a form of egotism,—that egotism which she has too much delicacy to cultivate. She is by no means sure that if being married to her beautiful baronet is not the ideal state she dreamed it, the weak point of the affair is not simply in her own presumption. It does n't express her condition, at present, to say that she is unhappy or disappointed, or that she has a sense of injury. All this is latent; meanwhile, what is obvious, is that she is bewildered,—she simply does n't understand; and her perplexity, to me, is unspeakably touching. She looks about her for some explanation, some light. She fixes her eyes on mine sometimes, and on those of other people, with a kind of searching dumbness, as if there were some chance that I—that they— may explain, may tell her what it is that has happened to her. I can explain very well, but not to her,—only to you!

III.

It was a brilliant match for Miss Bernardstone, who had no fortune at all, and all her friends were of the opinion that she had done very well After Easter she was in London with her people, and I saw a good deal of them, in fact, I rather cultivated them. They might perhaps even have thought me a little patronizing, if they had been given to thinking that sort of thing. But they were not; that is not in their line. English people are very apt to attribute motives,—some of them attribute much worse ones than we poor simpletons in America recognize, than we have even heard of! But that is only some of them; others don't, but take everything literally and genially. That was the case with the Bernardstones; you could be sure that on their way home, after dining with you, they would n't ask each other how in the world any one could call you pretty, or say that many people *did* believe, all the same, that you had poisoned your grandfather.

Lady Emily was exceedingly gratified at her daughter's engagement; of course she was very quiet about it, she did n't clap her hands or drag in Mr. Tester's name; but it was easy to see that she felt a kind of maternal peace, an abiding satisfaction. The young man behaved as well as possible, was constantly seen with Joscelind, and smiled down at her in the kindest, most protecting way. They looked beautiful together; you would have said it was a duty for people whose color matched so well to marry. Of course he was immensely taken up, and did n't come very often to see me; but he came sometimes, and when he sat there he had a look which I did n't understand at first. Presently I saw what it expressed; in my drawing-room he was off duty, he had no longer to sit up and play a part; he would lean back and rest and draw a long breath, and forget that the day of his execution was fixed. There was to be no indecent haste about the marriage; it was not to take place till after the session, at the end of August It puzzled me and rather distressed me. that his heart should n't be a little more in the matter; it seemed strange to be engaged to so charming a girl and yet go through with it as if it were simply a social duty. If one had n't been in love with her at first, one ought to have been at the end of a week or two. If Ambrose Tester was not (and to me he did n't pretend to be), he carried it off, as I have said, better than I should have expected. He was a gentleman, and he behaved like a gentleman, with the added punctilio, I think, of being sorry for his betrothed. But it was difficult to see what, in the long run, he could expect to make of such a position. If a man marries an ugly, unattractive woman for reasons of state, the thing is comparatively simple; it is understood between them, and he need have no remorse at not offering her a sentiment of which there has been no question. But when he picks out a charming creature to gratify his father and *les convenances*, it is not so easy to be happy in not being able to care for her. It seemed to me that it would have been much better for Ambrose Tester to bestow himself upon a girl who might have given him an excuse for tepidity. His wife should have been healthy but stupid, prolific but morose. Did he expect to continue not to be in love with Joscelind, or to conceal from her the mechanical nature of his attentions? It was difficult to see how he could wish to do the one or succeed in doing the other. Did he expect such a girl as that would be happy if he did n't love her? and did he think himself capable of being happy if it should turn out that she was miserable? If she should n't be miserable,—that is, if she should be indifferent, and, as they say, console herself, would he like that any better?

I asked myself all these questions and I should have liked to ask them of Mr. Tester; but I did n't, for after all he could n't have answered them. Poor young man! he did n't pry into things as I do; he was not analytic, like us Americans, as they say in reviews. He thought he was behaving remarkably well, and so he was—for a man; that was the strange part of it. It had been proper that in spite of his reluctance he should take a wife, and he had dutifully set about it. As a good thing is better for being well done, he had taken the best one he could possibly find. He was enchanted with—with his young lady, you might ask? Not in the least; with himself; that is the sort of person a man is! Their virtues are more dangerous than their vices, and Heaven preserve you when they want to keep a promise! It is never a promise to *you*, you will notice. A man will sacrifice a woman to live as a gentleman should, and then ask for your sympathy—for *him*! And I don't speak of the bad ones, but of the good. They, after all, are the worst Ambrose Tester, as I say, did n't go into these details, but synthetic as he might be, was conscious that his position was false. He felt that sooner or later, and rather sooner than later, he would have to make it true,—a process that could n't possibly be agreeable. He would really have to make up his mind to care for his wife or not to care for her. What would Lady Vandeleur say to one alternative, and what would little Joscelind say to the other? That is what it was to have a pertinacious father and to be an accommodating son. With me, it was easy for Ambrose Tester to be superficial, for, as I tell you, if I did n't wish to engage him, I did n't wish to disengage him, and I did n't insist Lady Vandeleur insisted, I was afraid; to be with her was of course very complicated; even more than Miss Bernardstone she must have made him feel that his position was false. I must add that he once mentioned to me that she had told him he ought to marry. At any rate, it is an immense thing to be a pleasant fellow. Our young fellow was so universally pleasant that of course his *fiancée* came in for her share. So did Lady Emily, suffused with hope, which made her pinker than ever; she told me he sent flowers even to her. One day in the Park, I was riding early; the Row was almost empty. I came up behind a lady and gentleman who were walking their horses, close to each other, side by side In a moment I recognized her, but not before seeing that nothing could have been more benevolent than the way Ambrose Tester was bending over his future wife. If he struck me as a lover at that moment, of course he struck her so. But that is n't the way they ride to-day.

IV.

One day, about the end of June, he came in to see me when I had two or three other visitors; you know that even at that season I am almost always at home from six to seven. He had not been three minutes in the room before I saw that he was different,—different from what he had been the last time, and I guessed that something had happened in relation to his marriage. My visitors did n't, unfortunately, and they stayed and stayed until I was afraid he would have to go away without telling me what, I was sure, he had come for. But he sat them out; I think that by exception they did n't find him pleasant. After we were alone he abused them a little, and then he said, "Have you heard about Vandeleur? He 's very ill. She's awfully anxious." I had n't heard, and I told him so, asking a question or two; then my inquiries ceased, my breath almost failed me, for I had become aware of something very strange. The way he looked at me when he told me his news was a full confession,—a confession so full that I had needed a moment to take it in. He was not too strong a man to be taken by surprise,—not so strong but that in the presence of an unexpected occasion his first movement was to look about for a little help. I venture to call it help, the sort of thing he came to me for on that summer afternoon. It is always help when a woman who is not an idiot lets an embarrassed man take up her time. If he too is not an idiot, that does n't diminish the service; on the contrary his superiority to the average helps him to profit. Ambrose Tester had said to me more than once, in the past, that he was capable of telling me things, because I was an American, that he would n't confide to his own people. He had proved it before this, as I have hinted, and I must say that being an American, with him, was sometimes a questionable honor. I don't know whether he thinks us more discreet and more sympathetic (if he keeps up the system: he has abandoned it with me), or only more insensible, more proof against shocks; but it is certain that, like some other Englishmen I have known, he has appeared, in delicate cases, to think I would take a comprehensive view. When I have inquired into the grounds of this discrimination in our favor, he has contented himself with

saying, in the British-cursory manner, "Oh, I don't know; you are different!"
I remember he remarked once that our impressions were fresher. And I am
sure that now it was because of my nationality, in addition to other merits,
that he treated me to the confession I have just alluded to. At least I don't
suppose he would have gone about saying to people in general, "Her husband
will probably die, you know; then why should n't I marry Lady Vandeleur?"

That was the question which his whole expression and manner asked of
me, and of which, after a moment, I decided to take no notice. Why shouldn't
he? There was an excellent reason why he should n't It would just kill Joscelind
Bernardstone; that was why he should n't? The idea that he should be ready
to do it frightened me, and independent as he might think my point of view,
I had no desire to discuss such abominations. It struck me as an abomination
at this very first moment, and I have never wavered in my judgment of it. I
am always glad when I can take the measure of a thing as soon as I see it; it 's
a blessing to *feel* what we think, without balancing and comparing. It's a great
rest, too, and a great luxury. That, as I say, was the case with the feeling excited
in me by this happy idea of Ambrose Tester's. Cruel and wanton I thought
it then, cruel and wanton I thought it later, when it was pressed upon me.
I knew there were many other people that did n't agree with me, and I can
only hope for them that their conviction was as quick and positive as mine;
it all depends upon the way a thing strikes one. But I will add to this another
remark. I thought I was right then, and I still think I was right; but it strikes
me as a pity that I should have wished so much to be right Why could n't I be
content to be wrong; to renounce my influence (since I appeared to possess
the mystic article), and let my young friend do as he liked? As you observed
the situation at Doubleton, should n't you say it was of a nature to make one
wonder whether, after all, one did render a service to the younger lady?

At all events, as I say, I gave no sign to Ambrose Tester that I understood
him, that I guessed what he wished to come to. He got no satisfaction out of
me that day; it is very true that he made up for it later. I expressed regret at
Lord Vandeleur's illness, inquired into its nature and origin, hoped it would
n't prove as grave as might be feared, said I would call at the house and ask
about him, commiserated discreetly her ladyship, and in short gave my young

man no chance whatever. He knew that I had guessed his *arrière-pensée*, but he let me off for the moment, for which I was thankful; either because he was still ashamed of it, or because he supposed I was reserving myself for the catastrophe,—should it occur. Well, my dear, it did occur, at the end of ten days. Mr. Tester came to see me twice in that interval, each time to tell me that poor Vandeleur was worse; he had some internal inflammation which, in nine cases out of ten, is fatal. His wife was all devotion; she was with him night and day. I had the news from other sources as well; I leave you to imagine whether in London, at the height of the season, such a situation could fail to be considerably discussed. To the discussion as yet, however, I contributed little, and with Ambrose Tester nothing at all. I was still on my guard. I never admitted for a moment that it was possible there should be any change in his plans. By this time, I think, he had quite ceased to be ashamed of his idea, he was in a state almost of exaltation about it; but he was very angry with me for not giving him an opening.

As I look back upon the matter now, there is something almost amusing in the way we watched each other,—he thinking that I evaded his question only to torment him (he believed me, or pretended to believe me, capable of this sort of perversity), and I determined not to lose ground by betraying an insight into his state of mind which he might twist into an expression of sympathy. I wished to leave my sympathy where I had placed it, with Lady Emily and her daughter, of whom I continued, bumping against them at parties, to have some observation. They gave no signal of alarm; of course it would have been premature. The girl, I am sure, had no idea of the existence of a rival. How they had kept her in the dark I don't know; but it was easy to see she was too much in love to suspect or to criticise. With Lady Emily it was different; she was a woman of charity, but she touched the world at too many points not to feel its vibrations. However, the dear little woman planted herself firmly; to the eye she was still enough. It was not from Ambrose Tester that I first heard of Lord Vandeleur's death; it was announced, with a quarter of a column of "padding," in the *Times*. I have always known the *Times* was a wonderful journal, but this never came home to me so much as when it produced a quarter of a column about Lord Vandeleur. It was a triumph of word-spinning. If he had carried out his vocation, if he had been a tailor or a hatter (that's how I see him), there might have been something to say about him. But he missed his vocation, he missed everything but posthumous honors. I was so sure Ambrose Tester would come in that afternoon, and so sure he knew I should expect him, that I threw over an engagement on purpose. But he didn't come in, nor the next day, nor the next. There were two possible explanations of his absence. One was that he was giving all his time to consoling Lady Vandeleur; the other was that he was giving it all, as a blind, to Joscelind Bernardstone. Both proved incorrect, for when he at last turned up he told me he had been for a week in the country, at his father's. Sir Edmund also had been unwell; but he had pulled through better than poor Lord Vandeleur. I wondered at first whether his son had been talking over with him the question of a change of base; but guessed in a moment that he had not suffered this alarm. I don't think that Ambrose would have spared him if he had thought it necessary to give him warning; but he probably held that his father would have no ground for complaint so long as he should marry some one; would have no right to remonstrate if he simply transferred his contract. Lady Vandeleur had had two children (whom she had lost), and might, therefore, have others whom she should n't lose; that would have been a reply to nice discriminations on Sir Edmund's part.

V.

In reality, what the young man had been doing was thinking it over beneath his ancestral oaks and beeches. His countenance showed this,—showed it more than Miss Bernardstone could have liked. He looked like a man who was crossed, not like a man who was happy, in love. I was no more disposed than before to help him out with his plot, but at the end of ten minutes we were articulately discussing it. When I say *we* were, I mean he was; for I sat before him quite mute, at first, and amazed at the clearness with which, before his conscience, he had argued his case. He had persuaded himself that it was quite a simple matter to throw over poor Joscelind and keep himself free for the expiration of Lady Vandeleur's term of mourning. The deliberations of an impulsive man sometimes land him in strange countries. Ambrose Tester confided his plan to me as a tremendous secret. He professed to wish immensely to know how it appeared to me, and whether my woman's wit could n't discover for him some loophole big enough round, some honorable way of not keeping faith. Yet at the same time he seemed not to foresee that I should, of necessity, be simply horrified. Disconcerted and perplexed (a little), that he was prepared to find me; but if I had refused, as yet, to come to his assistance, he appeared to suppose it was only because of the real difficulty of suggesting to him that perfect pretext of which he was in want. He evidently counted upon me, however, for some illuminating proposal, and I think he would have liked to say to me, "You have always pretended to be a great friend of mine,"—I hadn't; the pretension was all on his side,—"and now is your chance to show it. Go to Joscelind and make her feel (women have a hundred ways of doing that sort of thing), that through Vandeleur's death the change in my situation is complete. If she is the girl I take her for, she will know what to do in the premises."

I was not prepared to oblige him to this degree, and I lost no time in telling him so, after my first surprise at seeing how definite his purpose had become. His contention, after all, was very simple. He had been in love with Lady Vandeleur for years, and was now more in love with her than ever. There had been no appearance of her being, within a calculable period, liberated by the death of her husband. This nobleman was—he didn't say what just then (it was too soon)—but he was only forty years old, and in such health and preservation as to make such a contingency infinitely remote. Under these circumstances, Ambrose had been driven, for the most worldly reasons—he was ashamed of them, pah!—into an engagement with a girl he did n't love, and did n't pretend to love. Suddenly the unexpected occurred; the woman he did love had become accessible to him, and all the relations of things were altered.

Why should n't he alter, too? Why should n't Miss Bernardstone alter, Lady Emily alter, and every one alter? It would be *wrong* in him to marry Joscelind in so changed a world;—a moment's consideration would certainly assure me of that. He could no longer carry out his part of the bargain, and the transaction must stop before it went any further. If Joscelind knew, she would be the first to recognize this, and the thing for her now was to know.

"Go and tell her, then, if you are so sure of it," I said. "I wonder you have put it off so many days."

He looked at me with a melancholy eye. "Of course I know it's beastly awkward."

It was beastly awkward certainly; there I could quite agree with him, and this was the only sympathy he extracted from me. It was impossible to be less helpful, less merciful, to an embarrassed young man than I was on that occasion. But other occasions followed very quickly, on which Mr. Tester renewed his appeal with greater eloquence. He assured me that it was torture to be with his intended, and every hour that he did n't break off committed him more deeply and more fatally. I repeated only once my previous question,—asked him only once why then he did n't tell her he had changed his mind. The inquiry was idle, was even unkind, for my young man was in a very tight place. He did n't tell her, simply because he could n't, in spite of the anguish of feeling that his chance to right himself was rapidly passing away. When I asked him if Joscelind appeared to have guessed nothing, he broke out, "How in the world can she guess, when I am so kind to her? I am so sorry for her, poor little wretch, that I can't help being nice to her. And from the moment I am nice to her she thinks it's all right."

I could see perfectly what he meant by that, and I liked him more for this little generosity than I disliked him for his nefarious scheme. In fact, I did n't dislike him at all when I saw what an influence my judgment would have on him. I very soon gave him the full benefit of it. I had thought over his case with all the advantages of his own presentation of it, and it was impossible for me to see how he could decently get rid of the girl. That, as I have said, had been my original opinion, and quickened reflection only confirmed it. As I have also said, I had n't in the least recommended him to become engaged; but once he had done so I recommended him to abide by it. It was all very well being in love with Lady Vandeleur; he might be in love with her, but he had n't promised to marry her. It was all very well not being in love with Miss Bernardstone; but, as it happened, he had promised to marry her, and in my country a gentleman was supposed to keep such promises. If it was a question of keeping them only so long as was convenient, where would any of us be? I assure you I became very eloquent and moral,—yes, moral, I maintain the word, in spite of your perhaps thinking (as you are very capable of doing) that I ought to have advised him in just the opposite sense. It was not a question of love, but of marriage, for he had never promised to love poor Joscelind. It was useless his saying it was dreadful to marry without love; he knew that he thought it, and the people he lived with thought it, nothing of the kind. Half his friends had married on those terms. "Yes, and a pretty sight their private life presented!" That might be, but it was the first time I had ever heard him say it. A fortnight before he had been quite ready to do like the others. I knew what I thought, and I suppose I expressed it with some clearness, for my arguments made him still more uncomfortable, unable as he was either to accept them or to act in contempt of them. Why he should have cared so much for my opinion is a mystery I can't elucidate; to understand my little story, you must simply swallow it. That he did care is proved by the exasperation with which he suddenly broke out, "Well, then, as I understand you, what you recommend me is to marry Miss Bernardstone, and carry on an intrigue with Lady Vandeleur!"

He knew perfectly that I recommended nothing of the sort, and he must have been very angry to indulge in this *boutade*. He told me that other people did n't think as I did—that every one was of the opinion that between a woman he did n't love and a woman he had adored for years it was a plain moral duty not to hesitate. "Don't hesitate then!" I exclaimed; but I did n't get rid of him with this, for he returned to the charge more than once (he came to me so often that I thought he must neglect both his other alternatives), and let me know again that the voice of society was quite against my view. You will doubtless be surprised at such an intimation that he had taken "society" into his confidence, and wonder whether he went about asking people whether they thought he might back out. I can't tell you exactly, but I know that for some weeks his dilemma was a great deal talked about. His friends perceived he was at the parting of the roads, and many of them had no difficulty in saying which one *they* would take. Some observers thought he ought to do nothing, to leave things as they were. Others took very high ground and discoursed upon the sanctity of love and the wickedness of really deceiving the girl, as that would be what it would amount to (if he should lead her to the altar). Some held that it was too late to escape, others maintained that it is never too late. Some thought Miss Bernardstone very much to be pitied; some reserved their compassion for Ambrose Tester; others, still, lavished it upon Lady Vandeleur.

The prevailing opinion, I think, was that he ought to obey the promptings of his heart—London cares so much for the heart! Or is it that London is simply ferocious, and always prefers the spectacle that is more entertaining? As it would prolong the drama for the young man to throw over Miss Bernardstone, there was a considerable readiness to see the poor girl sacrificed. She was like a Christian maiden in the Roman arena. That is what Ambrose Tester meant by telling me that public opinion was on his side. I don't think he chattered about his quandary, but people, knowing his situation, guessed what was going on in his mind, and he on his side guessed what they said. London discussions might as well go on in the whispering-gallery of St. Paul's. I could of course do only one thing,—I could but reaffirm my conviction that the Roman attitude, as I may call it, was cruel, was falsely sentimental. This naturally did n't help him as he wished to be helped,—did n't remove the obstacle to his marrying in a year or two Lady Vandeleur. Yet he continued to look to me for inspiration,—I must say it at the cost of making him appear a very feeble-minded gentleman. There was a moment when I thought him capable of an oblique movement, of temporizing with a view to escape. If he succeeded in postponing his marriage long enough, the Bernardstones would throw *him* over, and I suspect that for a day he entertained the idea of fixing this responsibility on them. But he was too honest and too generous to do so for longer, and his destiny was staring him in the face when an accident gave him a momentary relief. General Bernardstone died, after an illness as sudden and short as that which had carried off Lord Vandeleur; his wife and daughter were plunged into mourning and immediately retired into the country. A week later we heard that the girl's marriage would be put off for several months,—partly on account of her mourning, and partly because her mother, whose only companion she had now become, could not bear to part with her at the time originally fixed and actually so near. People of course looked at each other,—said it was the beginning of the end, a "dodge" of Ambrose Tester's. I wonder they did n't accuse him of poisoning the poor old general. I know to a certainty that he had nothing to do with the delay, that the proposal came from Lady Emily, who, in her bereavement, wished, very naturally, to keep a few months longer the child she was going to lose forever. It must be said, in justice to her prospective son-in-law, that he was capable either of resigning himself or of frankly (with however many blushes) telling Joscelind he could n't keep his agreement, but was not capable of trying to wriggle out of his difficulty. The plan of simply telling Joscelind he couldn't,—this was the one he had fixed upon as the best, and this was the one of which I remarked to him that it had a defect which should be counted against its advantages. The defect was that it would kill Joscelind on the spot.

I think he believed me, and his believing me made this unexpected respite very welcome to him. There was no knowing what might happen in the interval, and he passed a large part of it in looking for an issue. And yet, at the same time, he kept up the usual forms with the girl whom in his heart he had renounced. I was told more than once (for I had lost sight of the pair during the summer and autumn) that these forms were at times very casual, that he neglected Miss Bernardstone most flagrantly, and had quite resumed his old intimacy with Lady Vandeleur. I don't exactly know what was meant by this, for she spent the first three months of her widowhood in complete seclusion, in her own old house in Norfolk, where he certainly was not staying with her. I believe he stayed some time, for the partridge shooting, at a place a few miles off. It came to my ears that if Miss Bernardstone did n't take the hint it was because she was determined to stick to him through thick and thin. She never offered to let him off, and I was sure she never would; but I was equally sure that, strange as it may appear, he had not ceased to be nice to her. I have never exactly understood why he didn't hate her, and I am convinced that he was not a comedian in his conduct to her,—he was only a good fellow. I have spoken of the satisfaction that Sir Edmund took in his daughter-in-law that was to be; he delighted in looking at her, longed for her when she was out of his sight, and had her, with her mother, staying with him in the country for weeks together. If Ambrose was not so constantly at her side as he might have been, this deficiency was covered by his father's devotion to her, by her appearance of being already one of the family. Mr. Tester was away as he might be away if they were already married.

VI.

In October I met him at Doubleton; we spent three days there together. He was enjoying his respite, as he didn't scruple to tell me; and he talked to me a great deal—as usual—about Lady Vandeleur. He did n't mention Joscelind's name, except by implication in this assurance of how much he valued his weeks of grace.

"Do you mean to say that, under the circumstances, Lady Vandeleur is willing to marry you?"

I made this inquiry more expressively, doubtless, than before; for when we had talked of the matter then he had naturally spoken of her consent as a simple contingency. It was contingent upon the lapse of the first months of her bereavement; it was not a question he could begin to press a few days after her husband's death.

"Not immediately, of course; but if I wait, I think so." That, I remember, was his answer.

"If you wait till you get rid of that poor girl, of course."

"She knows nothing about that,—it's none of her business."

"Do you mean to say she does n't know you are engaged?"

"How should she know it, how should she believe it, when she sees how I love her?" the young man exclaimed; but he admitted afterwards that he had not deceived her, and that she rendered full justice to the motives that had determined him. He thought he could answer for it that she would marry him some day or other.

"Then she is a very cruel woman," I said, "and I should like, if you please, to hear no more about her." He protested against this, and, a month later, brought her up again, for a purpose. The purpose, you will see, was a very strange one indeed. I had then come back to town; it was the early part of December. I supposed he was hunting, with his own hounds; but he appeared one afternoon in my drawing-room and told me I should do him a great favor if I would go and see Lady Vandeleur.

"Go and see her? Where do you mean, in Norfolk?"

"She has come up to London—did n't you know it? She has a lot of business. She will be kept here till Christmas; I wish you would go."

"Why should I go?" I asked. "Won't you be kept here till Christmas too, and is n't that company enough for her?"

"Upon my word, you are cruel," he said, "and it's a great shame of you, when a man is trying to do his duty and is behaving like a saint."

"Is that what you call saintly, spending all your time with Lady Vandeleur? I will tell you whom I think a saint, if you would like to know."

"You need n't tell me; I know it better than you. I haven't a word to say against her; only she is stupid and hasn't any perceptions. If I am stopping a bit in London you don't understand why; it's as if you had n't any perceptions either! If I am here for a few days, I know what I am about."

"Why should I understand?" I asked,—not very candidly, because I should have been glad to. "It's your own affair; you know what you are about, as you say, and of course you have counted the cost."

"What cost do you mean? It's a pretty cost, I can tell you." And then he tried to explain—if I would only enter into it, and not be so suspicious. He was in London for the express purpose of breaking off.

"Breaking off what,—your engagement?"

"No, no, damn my engagement,—the other thing. My acquaintance, my relations—"

"Your intimacy with Lady Van—?" It was not very gentle, but I believe I burst out laughing. "If this is the way you break off, pray what would you do to keep up?"

He flushed, and looked both foolish and angry, for of course it was not very difficult to see my point. But he was—in a very clumsy manner of his own—trying to cultivate a good conscience, and he was getting no credit for it. "I suppose I may be allowed to look at her! It's a matter we have to talk over. One does n't drop such a friend in half an hour."

"One does n't drop her at all, unless one has the strength to make a sacrifice."

"It's easy for you to talk of sacrifice. You don't know what she is!" my visitor cried.

"I think I know what she is not. She is not a friend, as you call her, if she encourages you in the wrong, if she does n't help you. No, I have no patience with her," I declared; "I don't like her, and I won't go to see her!"

Mr. Tester looked at me a moment, as if he were too vexed to trust himself to speak. He had to make an effort not to say something rude. That effort however, he was capable of making, and though he held his hat as if he were going to walk out of the house, he ended by staying, by putting it down again, by leaning his head, with his elbows on his knees, in his hands, and groaning out that he had never heard of anything so impossible, and that he was the most wretched man in England. I was very sorry for him, and of course I told him so; but privately I did n't think he stood up to his duty as he ought. I said to him, however, that if he would give me his word of honor that he would not abandon Miss Bernardstone, there was no trouble I would n't take to be of use to him. I did n't think Lady Vandeleur *was* behaving well. He must allow me to repeat that; but if going to see her would give him any pleasure (of course there was no question of pleasure for *her*) I would go fifty times. I could n't imagine how it would help him, but I would do it as I would do anything else he asked me. He did n't give me his word of honor, but he said quietly, "*I* shall go straight; you need n't be afraid;" and as he spoke there was honor enough in his face. This left an opening, of course, for another catastrophe. There might be further postponements, and poor Lady Emily, indignant for the first time in her life, might declare that her daughter's situation had become intolerable and that they withdrew from the engagement. But this was too odious a chance, and I accepted Mr. Tester's assurance. He told me that the good I could do by going to see Lady Vandeleur was that it would cheer her up, in that dreary, big house in Upper Brook Street, where she was absolutely alone, with horrible overalls on the furniture, and newspapers—actually newspapers—on the mirrors. She was seeing no one, there was no one to see; but he knew she would see me. I asked him if she knew, then, he was to speak to me of coming, and whether I might allude to him, whether it was not too delicate. I shall never forget his answer to this, nor the tone in which he made it, blushing a little, and looking away. "Allude to me? Rather!" It was not the most fatuous speech I had ever heard; it had the effect of being the most modest; and it gave me an odd idea, and especially a new one, of the condition in which, at any time, one might be destined to find Lady Vandeleur. If she, too, were engaged in a struggle with her conscience (in this light they were an edifying pair!) it had perhaps changed her considerably, made her more approachable; and I reflected, ingeniously, that it probably had a humanizing effect upon her. Ambrose Tester did n't go away after I had told him that I would comply with his request. He lingered, fidgeting with his stick and gloves, and I perceived that he had more to tell me, and that the real reason why he wished me to go and see Lady Vandeleur was not that she had newspapers on her mirrors. He came out with it at last, for that "Rather!" of his (with the way I took it) had broken the ice.

"You say you don't think she behaved well" (he naturally wished to defend her). "But I dare say you don't understand her position. Perhaps you would n't behave any better in her place."

"It's very good of you to imagine me there!" I remarked, laughing.

"It's awkward for me to say. One doesn't want to dot one's i's to that extent."

"She would be delighted to marry you. That's not such a mystery."

"Well, she likes me awfully," Mr. Tester said, looking like a handsome child. "It's not all on one side; it's on both. That's the difficulty."

"You mean she won't let you go?—she holds you fast?"

But the poor fellow had, in delicacy, said enough, and at this he jumped up. He stood there a moment, smoothing his hat; then he broke out again: "Please do this. Let her know—make her feel. You can bring it in, you know." And here he paused, embarrassed.

"What can I bring in, Mr. Tester? That's the difficulty, as you say."

"What you told me the other day. You know. What you have told me before."

"What I have told you—?"

"That it would put an end to Joscelind! If you can't work round to it, what's the good of being—you?" And with this tribute to my powers he took his departure.

VII.

It was all very well of him to be so flattering, but I really did n't see myself talking in that manner to Lady Vandeleur. I wondered why he didn't give her this information himself, and what particular value it could have as coming from me. Then I said to myself that of course he *had* mentioned to her the truth I had impressed upon him (and which by this time he had evidently taken home), but that to enable it to produce its full effect upon Lady Yandeleur the further testimony of a witness more independent was required. There was nothing for me but to go and see her, and I went the next day, fully conscious that to execute Mr. Tester's commission I should have either to find myself very brave or to find her strangely confidential; and fully prepared, also, not to be admitted. But she received me, and the house in Upper Brook Street was as dismal as Ambrose Tester had represented it. The December fog (the afternoon was very dusky) seemed to pervade the muffled rooms, and her ladyship's pink lamplight to waste itself in the brown atmosphere. He had mentioned to me that the heir to the title (a cousin of her husband), who had left her unmolested for several months, was now taking possession of everything, so that what kept her in town was the business of her "turning out," and certain formalities connected with her dower. This was very ample, and the large provision made for her included the London house. She was very gracious on this occasion, but she certainly had remarkably little to say. Still, she was different, or at any rate (having taken that hint), I saw her differently. I saw, indeed, that I had never quite done her justice, that I had exaggerated her stiffness, attributed to her a kind of conscious grandeur which was in reality much more an accident of her appearance, of her figure, than a quality of her character. Her appearance is as grand as you know, and on the day I speak of, in her simplified mourning, under those vaguely gleaming *lambris*, she looked as beautiful as a great white lily. She is very simple and good-natured; she will never make an advance, but she will always respond to one, and I saw, that evening, that the way to get on with her was to treat her as if she were not too imposing. I saw also that, with her nun-like robes and languid eyes, she was a woman who might be immensely in love. All the same, we hadn't much to say to each other. She remarked that it was very kind of me to come, that she wondered how I could endure London at that season, that she had taken a drive and found the Park too dreadful, that she would ring for some more tea if I did n't like what she had given me. Our conversation wandered, stumbling a little, among these platitudes, but no allusion was made on either side to Ambrose Tester. Nevertheless, as I have said, she was different, though it was not till I got home that I phrased to myself what I had detected.

Then, recalling her white face, and the deeper, stranger expression of her beautiful eyes, I entertained myself with the idea that she was under the influence of "suppressed exaltation." The more I thought of her the more she appeared to me not natural; wound up, as it were, to a calmness beneath which there was a deal of agitation. This would have been nonsense if I had not, two days afterwards, received a note from her which struck me as an absolutely "exalted" production. Not superficially, of course; to the casual eye it would have been perfectly commonplace. But this was precisely its peculiarity, that Lady Vandeleur should have written me a note which had no apparent point save that she should like to see me again, a desire for which she did succeed in assigning a reason. She reminded me that she was paying no calls, and she hoped I wouldn't stand on ceremony, but come in very soon again, she had enjoyed my visit so much. We had not been on note-writing terms, and there was nothing in that visit to alter our relations; moreover, six months before, she would not have dreamed of addressing me in that way. I was doubly convinced, therefore, that she was passing through a crisis, that she was not in her normal state of nerves. Mr. Tester had not reappeared since the occasion I have described at length, and I thought it possible he had been capable of the bravery of leaving town. I had, however, no fear of meeting him in Upper Brook Street; for, according to my theory of his relations with Lady Vaudeleur, he regularly spent his evenings with her, it being clear to me that they must dine together. I could answer her note only by going to see her the next day, when I found abundant confirmation of that idea about the crisis. I must confess to you in advance that I have never really understood her behavior,—never understood why she should have taken me so suddenly—

with whatever reserves, and however much by implication merely—into her confidence. All I can say is that this is an accident to which one is exposed with English people, who, in my opinion, and contrary to common report, are the most demonstrative, the most expansive, the most gushing in the world. I think she felt rather isolated at this moment, and she had never had many intimates of her own sex. That sex, as a general thing, disapproved of her proceedings during the last few months, held that she was making Joscelind Bernardstone suffer too cruelly. She possibly felt the weight of this censure, and at all events was not above wishing some one to know that whatever injury had fallen upon the girl to whom Mr. Tester had so stupidly engaged himself, had not, so far as she was concerned, been wantonly inflicted. I was there, I was more or less aware of her situation, and I would do as well as any one else.

She seemed really glad to see me, but she was very nervous. Nevertheless, nearly half an hour elapsed, and I was still wondering whether she had sent for me only to discuss the question of how a London house whose appointments had the stamp of a debased period (it had been thought very handsome in 1850) could be "done up" without being made æsthetic. I forget what satisfaction I gave her on this point; I was asking myself how I could work round in the manner prescribed by Joscelind's intended. At the last, however, to my extreme surprise, Lady Vandeleur herself relieved me of this effort.

"I think you know Mr. Tester rather well," she remarked, abruptly, irrelevantly, and with a face' more conscious of the bearings of things than any I had ever seen her wear. On my confessing to such an acquaintance, she mentioned that Mr. Tester (who had been in London a few days—perhaps I had seen him) had left town and would n't come back for several weeks. This, for the moment, seemed to be all she had to communicate; but she sat looking at me from the corner of her sofa as if she wished me to profit in some way by the opportunity she had given me. Did she want help from outside, this proud, inscrutable woman, and was she reduced to throwing out signals of distress? Did she wish to be protected against herself,—applauded for such efforts as she had already made? I didn't rush forward, I was not precipitate, for I felt that now, surely, I should be able at my convenience to execute my commission. What concerned me was not to prevent Lady Vandeleur's marrying Mr. Tester, but to prevent Mr. Tester's marrying her. In a few moments—with the same irrelevance—she announced to me that he wished to, and asked whether I didn't know it I saw that this was my chance, and instantly, with extreme energy, I exclaimed,—

"Ah, for Heaven's sake don't listen to him! It would kill Miss Bernardstone!"

The tone of my voice made her color a little, and she repeated, "Miss Bernardstone?"

"The girl he is engaged to,—or has been,—don't you know? Excuse me, I thought every one knew."

"Of course I know he is dreadfully entangled. He was fairly hunted down." Lady Vandeleur was silent a moment, and then she added, with a strange smile, "Fancy, in such a situation, his wanting to marry me!"

"Fancy!" I replied. I was so struck with the oddity of her telling me her secrets that for the moment my indignation did not come to a head,—my indignation, I mean, at her accusing poor Lady Emily (and even the girl herself) of having "trapped" our friend. Later I said to myself that I supposed she was within her literal right in abusing her rival, if she was trying sincerely to give him up. "I don't know anything about his having been hunted down," I said; "but this I do know, Lady Vandeleur, I assure you, that if he should throw Joscelind over she would simply go out like that!" And I snapped my fingers.

Lady Vandeleur listened to this serenely enough; she tried at least to take the air of a woman who has no need of new arguments. "Do you know her very well?" she asked, as if she had been struck by my calling Miss Bernardstone by her Christian name.

"Well enough to like her very much." I was going to say "to pity her;" but I thought better of it.

"She must be a person of very little spirit. If a man were to jilt me, I don't think I should go out!" cried her ladyship with a laugh.

113

"Nothing is more probable than that she has not your courage or your wisdom. She may be weak, but she is passionately in love with him."

I looked straight into Lady Vandeleur's eyes as I said this, and I was conscious that it was a tolerably good description of my hostess.

"Do you think she would really die?" she asked in a moment.

"Die as if one should stab her with a knife. Some people don't believe in broken hearts," I continued. "I did n't till I knew Joscelind Bernardstone; then I felt that she had one that would n't be proof."

"One ought to live,—one ought always to live," said Lady Yandeleur; "and always to hold up one's head."

"Ah, I suppose that one ought n't to feel at all, if one wishes to be a great success."

"What do you call a great success?" she asked.

"Never having occasion to be pitied."

"Being pitied? That must be odious!" she said; and I saw that though she might wish for admiration, she would never wish for sympathy. Then, in a moment, she added that men, in her opinion, were very base,—a remark that was deep, but not, I think, very honest; that is, in so far as the purpose of it had been to give me the idea that Ambrose Tester had done nothing but press her, and she had done nothing but resist. They were very odd, the discrepancies in the statements of each of this pair; but it must be said for Lady Vandeleur that now that she had made up her mind (as I believed she had) to sacrifice herself, she really persuaded herself that she had not had a moment of weakness. She quite unbosomed herself, and I fairly assisted at her crisis. It appears that she had a conscience,—very much so, and even a high ideal of duty. She represented herself as moving heaven and earth to keep Ambrose Tester up to the mark, and you would never have guessed from what she told me that she had entertained ever so faintly the idea of marrying him. I am sure this was a dreadful perversion, but I forgave it on the score of that exaltation of which I have spoken. The things she said, and the way she said them, come back to me, and I thought that if she looked as handsome as that when she preached virtue to Mr. Tester, it was no wonder he liked the sermon to be going on perpetually.

"I dare say you know what old friends we are; but that does n't make any difference, does it? Nothing would induce me to marry him,—I have n't the smallest intention of marrying again. It is not a time for me to think of marrying, before his lordship has been dead six months. The girl is nothing to me; I know nothing about her, and I don't wish to know; but I should be very, very sorry if she were unhappy. He is the best friend I ever had, but I don't see that that's any reason I should marry him, do you?" Lady Vaudeleur appealed to me, but without waiting for my answers, asking advice in spite of herself, and then remembering it was beneath her dignity to appear to be in need of it. "I have told him that if he does n't act properly I shall never speak to him again. She's a charming girl, every one says, and I have no doubt she will make him perfectly happy. Men don't feel things like women, I think, and if they are coddled and flattered they forget the rest. I have no doubt she is very sufficient for all that. For me, at any rate, once I see a thing in a certain way, I must abide by that I think people are so dreadful,—they do such horrible things. They don't seem to think what one's duty may be. I don't know whether you think much about that, but really one must at times, don't you think so? Every one is so selfish, and then, when they have never made an effort or a sacrifice themselves, they come to you and talk such a lot of hypocrisy. I know so much better than any one else whether I should marry or not. But I don't mind telling you that I don't see why I should. I am not in such a bad position,—with my liberty and a decent maintenance."

In this manner she rambled on, gravely and communicatively, contradicting herself at times; not talking fast (she never did), but dropping one simple sentence, with an interval, after the other, with a certain richness of voice which always was part of the charm of her presence. She wished to be convinced against herself, and it was a comfort to her to hear herself argue. I was quite willing to be part of the audience, though I had to confine myself to very superficial remarks; for when I had said the event I feared would kill Miss Bernardstone I had said everything that was open to me. I had nothing to do with Lady Vandeleur's marrying, apart from that I probably disappointed her. She had caught a glimpse of the moral beauty of self-sacrifice, of a certain ideal of conduct (I imagine it was rather new to her), and would have been glad to elicit from me, as a person of some experience of life, an assurance that such joys are not insubstantial. I had no wish to wind her up to a spiritual ecstasy from which she would inevitably descend again, and I let her deliver herself according to her humor, without attempting to answer for it that she would find renunciation the road to bliss. I believed that if she should give up Mr. Tester she would suffer accordingly; but I did n't think that a reason for not giving him up. Before I left her she said to me that nothing would induce her to do anything that she did n't think right. "It would be no pleasure to me, don't you see? I should be always thinking that another way would have been better. Nothing would induce me,—nothing, nothing!"

VIII.

She protested too much, perhaps, but the event seemed to show that she was in earnest. I have described these two first visits of mine in some detail, but they were not the only ones I paid her. I saw her several times again, before she left town, and we became intimate, as London intimacies are measured. She ceased to protest (to my relief, for it made me nervous), she was very gentle, and gracious, and reasonable, and there was something in the way she looked and spoke that told me that for the present she found renunciation its own reward. So far, my scepticism was put to shame; her spiritual ecstasy maintained itself. If I could have foreseen then that it would maintain itself till the present hour I should have felt that Lady Vandeleur's moral nature is finer indeed than mine. I heard from her that Mr. Tester remained at his father's, and that Lady Emily and her daughter were also there. The day for the wedding had been fixed, and the preparations were going rapidly forward. Meanwhile—she didn't tell me, but I gathered it from things she dropped—she was in almost daily correspondence with the young man. I thought this a strange concomitant of his bridal arrangements; but apparently, henceforth, they were bent on convincing each other that the torch of virtue lighted their steps, and they couldn't convince each other too much. She intimated to me that she had now effectually persuaded him (always by letter), that he would fail terribly if he should try to found his happiness on an injury done to another, and that of course she could never be happy (in a union with him), with the sight of his wretchedness before her. That a good deal of correspondence should be required to elucidate this is perhaps after all not remarkable. One day, when I was sitting with her (it was just before she left town), she suddenly burst into tears. Before we parted I said to her that there were several women in London I liked very much,—that was common enough,—but for her I had a positive respect, and that was rare. My respect continues still, and it sometimes makes me furious.

About the middle of January Ambrose Tester reappeared in town. He told me he came to bid me good-by. He was going to be beheaded. It was no use saying that old relations would be the same after a man was married; they would be different, everything would be different. I had wanted him to marry, and now I should see how I liked it He did n't mention that I had also wanted him not to marry, and I was sure that if Lady Vandeleur had become his wife, she would have been a much greater impediment to our harmless friendship than Joscelind Bernardstone would ever be. It took me but a short time to observe that he was in very much the same condition as Lady Vandeleur. He was finding how sweet it is to renounce, hand in hand with one we love. Upon him, too, the peace of the Lord had descended. He spoke of his father's delight at the nuptials being so near at hand; at the festivities that would take place in Dorsetshire when he should bring home his bride. The only allusion he made to what we had talked of the last time we were together was to exclaim suddenly, "How can I tell you how easy she has made it? She is so sweet, so noble. She really is a perfect creature!" I took for granted that he was talking of his future wife, but in a moment, as we were at cross-purposes, perceived that he meant Lady Vandeleur. This seemed to me really ominous. It stuck in my mind after he had left me. I was half tempted to write him a note, to say, "There is, after all, perhaps, something worse than your jilting Miss Bernardstone would be; and that is the danger that your rupture with Lady Vandeleur may become more of a bond than your marrying her would have been For Heaven's sake, let your sacrifice *be* a sacrifice; keep it in its proper place!"

Of course I did n't write; even the slight responsibility I had already incurred began to frighten me, and I never saw Mr. Tester again till he was the husband of Joscelind Bernardstone. They have now been married some four years; they have two children, the eldest of whom is, as he should be, a boy. Sir Edmund waited till his grandson had made good his place in the world, and then, feeling it was safe, he quietly, genially surrendered his trust. He died, holding the hand of his daughter-in-law, and giving it doubtless a pressure which was an injunction to be brave. I don't know what he thought of the success of his plan for his son; but perhaps, after all, he saw nothing amiss, for Joscelind is the last woman in the world to have troubled him with her sorrows. From him, no doubt, she successfully concealed that bewilderment on which I have touched. You see I speak of her sorrows as if they were a matter of common recognition; certain it is that any one who meets her must see that she does n't pass her life in joy. Lady Vandeleur, as you know, has never married again; she is still the most beautiful widow in England. She enjoys the esteem of every one, as well as the approbation of her conscience, for every one knows the sacrifice she made, knows that she was even more in love with Sir Ambrose than he was with her. She goes out again, of course, as of old, and she constantly meets the baronet and his wife. She is supposed to be even "very nice" to Lady Tester, and she certainly treats her with exceeding civility. But you know (or perhaps you don't know) all the deadly things that, in London, may lie beneath that method. I don't in the least mean that Lady Vandeleur has any deadly intentions; she is a very good woman, and I am sure that in her heart she thinks she lets poor Joscelind off very easily. But the result of the whole situation is that Joscelind is in dreadful fear of her, for how can she help seeing that she has a very peculiar power over her husband? There couldn't have been a better occasion for observing the three together (if together it may be called, when Lady Tester is so completely outside), than those two days of ours at Doubleton. That's a house where they have met more than once before; I think she and Sir Ambrose like it. By "she" I mean, as he used to mean, Lady Vandeleur. You saw how Lady Tester was absolutely white with uneasiness. What can she do when she meets everywhere the implication that if two people in our time have distinguished themselves for their virtue, it is her husband and Lady Vandeleur? It is my impression that this pair are exceedingly happy. His marriage *has* made a difference, and I see him much less frequently and less intimately. But when I meet him I notice in him a kind of emanation of quiet bliss. Yes, they are certainly in felicity, they have trod the clouds together, they have soared into the blue, and they wear in their faces the glory of those altitudes. They encourage, they cheer, inspire, sustain, each other, remind each other that they have chosen the better part Of course they have to meet for this purpose, and their interviews are filled, I am sure, with its sanctity. He holds up his head, as a man may who on a very critical occasion behaved like a perfect gentleman. It is only poor Joscelind that droops. Have n't I explained to you now why she does n't understand?

About Author

Henry James OM (15 April 1843 – 28 February 1916) was an American-British author regarded as a key transitional figure between literary realism and literary modernism, and is considered by many to be among the greatest novelists in the English language. He was the son of Henry James Sr. and the brother of renowned philosopher and psychologist William James and diarist Alice James.

He is best known for a number of novels dealing with the social and marital interplay between émigré Americans, English people, and continental Europeans. Examples of such novels include The Portrait of a Lady, The Ambassadors, and The Wings of the Dove. His later works were increasingly experimental. In describing the internal states of mind and social dynamics of his characters, James often made use of a style in which ambiguous or contradictory motives and impressions were overlaid or juxtaposed in the discussion of a character's psyche. For their unique ambiguity, as well as for other aspects of their composition, his late works have been compared to impressionist painting.

His novella The Turn of the Screw has garnered a reputation as the most analysed and ambiguous ghost story in the English language and remains his most widely adapted work in other media. He also wrote a number of other highly regarded ghost stories and is considered one of the greatest masters of the field.

James published articles and books of criticism, travel, biography, autobiography, and plays. Born in the United States, James largely relocated to Europe as a young man and eventually settled in England, becoming a British subject in 1915, one year before his death. James was nominated for the Nobel Prize in Literature in 1911, 1912 and 1916.

Life

Early years, 1843–1883

James was born at 2 Washington Place in New York City on 15 April 1843. His parents were Mary Walsh and Henry James Sr. His father was intelligent and steadfastly congenial. He was a lecturer and philosopher who had inherited independent means from his father, an Albany banker and investor. Mary came from a wealthy family long settled in New York City. Her sister Katherine lived with her adult family for an extended period of time. Henry Jr. had three brothers, William, who was one year his senior, and younger brothers Wilkinson (Wilkie) and Robertson. His younger sister was Alice. Both of his parents were of Irish and Scottish descent.

The family first lived in Albany, at 70 N. Pearl St., and then moved to Fourteenth Street in New York City when James was still a young boy. His education was calculated by his father to expose him to many influences, primarily scientific and philosophical; it was described by Percy Lubbock, the editor of his selected letters, as "extraordinarily haphazard and promiscuous." James did not share the usual education in Latin and Greek classics. Between 1855 and 1860, the James' household traveled to London, Paris, Geneva, Boulogne-sur-Mer and Newport, Rhode Island, according to the father's current interests and publishing ventures, retreating to the United States when funds were low. Henry studied primarily with tutors and briefly attended schools while the family traveled in Europe. Their longest stays were in France, where Henry began to feel at home and became fluent in French. He was afflicted with a stutter, which seems to have manifested itself only when he spoke English; in French, he did not stutter.

In 1860 the family returned to Newport. There Henry became a friend of the painter John La Farge, who introduced him to French literature, and in particular, to Balzac. James later called Balzac his "greatest master," and said that he had learned more about the craft of fiction from him than from anyone else.

In the autumn of 1861 Henry received an injury, probably to his back, while fighting a fire. This injury, which resurfaced at times throughout his life, made him unfit for military service in the American Civil War.

In 1864 the James family moved to Boston, Massachusetts to be near William, who had enrolled first in the Lawrence Scientific School at Harvard and then in the medical school. In 1862 Henry attended Harvard Law School, but realised that he was not interested in studying law. He pursued his interest in literature and associated with authors and critics William Dean Howells and Charles Eliot Norton in Boston and Cambridge, formed lifelong friendships with Oliver Wendell Holmes Jr., the future Supreme Court Justice, and with James and Annie Fields, his first professional mentors.

His first published work was a review of a stage performance, "Miss Maggie Mitchell in Fanchon the Cricket," published in 1863. About a year later, A Tragedy of Error, his first short story, was published anonymously. James's first payment was for an appreciation of Sir Walter Scott's novels, written for the North American Review. He wrote fiction and non-fiction pieces for The Nation and Atlantic Monthly, where Fields was editor. In 1871 he published his first novel, Watch and Ward, in serial form in the Atlantic Monthly. The novel was later published in book form in 1878.

During a 14-month trip through Europe in 1869–70 he met Ruskin, Dickens, Matthew Arnold, William Morris, and George Eliot. Rome impressed him profoundly. "Here I am then in the Eternal City," he wrote to his brother William. "At last—for the first time—I live!" He attempted to support himself as a freelance writer in Rome, then secured a position as Paris correspondent for the New York Tribune, through the influence of its editor John Hay. When these efforts failed he returned to New York City. During 1874 and 1875 he published Transatlantic Sketches, A Passionate Pilgrim, and Roderick Hudson. During this early period in his career he was influenced by Nathaniel Hawthorne.

In 1869 he settled in London. There he established relationships with Macmillan and other publishers, who paid for serial installments that they would later publish in book form. The audience for these serialized novels was largely made up of middle-class women, and James struggled to fashion serious literary work within the strictures imposed by editors' and publishers' notions of what was suitable for young women to read. He lived in rented rooms but was able to join gentlemen's clubs that had libraries and where he could entertain male friends. He was introduced to English society by Henry Adams and Charles Milnes Gaskell, the latter introducing him to the Travellers' and the Reform Clubs.

In the fall of 1875 he moved to the Latin Quarter of Paris. Aside from two trips to America, he spent the next three decades—the rest of his life—in Europe. In Paris he met Zola, Alphonse Daudet, Maupassant, Turgenev, and others. He stayed in Paris only a year before moving to London.

In England he met the leading figures of politics and culture. He continued to be a prolific writer, producing The American (1877), The Europeans (1878), a revision of Watch and Ward (1878), French Poets and Novelists (1878), Hawthorne (1879), and several shorter works of fiction. In 1878 Daisy Miller established his fame on both sides of the Atlantic. It drew notice perhaps mostly because it depicted a woman whose behavior is outside the social norms of Europe. He also began his first masterpiece, The Portrait of a Lady, which would appear in 1881.

In 1877 he first visited Wenlock Abbey in Shropshire, home of his friend Charles Milnes Gaskell whom he had met through Henry Adams. He was much inspired by the darkly romantic Abbey and the surrounding countryside, which features in his essay Abbeys and Castles. In particular the gloomy monastic fishponds behind the Abbey are said to have inspired the lake in The Turn of the Screw.

While living in London, James continued to follow the careers of the "French realists", Émile Zola in particular. Their stylistic methods influenced his own work in the years to come. Hawthorne's influence on him faded during this period, replaced by George Eliot and Ivan Turgenev. 1879–1882 saw the publication of The Europeans, Washington Square, Confidence, and The Portrait of a Lady. He visited America in 1882–1883, then returned to London.

The period from 1881 to 1883 was marked by several losses. His mother died in 1881, followed by his father a few months later, and then by his brother Wilkie. Emerson, an old family friend, died in 1882. His friend Turgenev died in 1883.

Middle years, 1884–1897

In 1884 James made another visit to Paris. There he met again with Zola, Daudet, and Goncourt. He had been following the careers of the French "realist" or "naturalist" writers, and was increasingly influenced by them. In 1886, he published The Bostonians and The Princess Casamassima, both influenced by the French writers he'd studied assiduously. Critical reaction and sales were poor. He wrote to Howells that the books had hurt his career rather than helped because they had "reduced the desire, and demand, for my productions to zero". During this time he became friends with Robert Louis Stevenson, John Singer Sargent, Edmund Gosse, George du Maurier, Paul Bourget, and Constance Fenimore Woolson. His third novel from the 1880s was The Tragic Muse. Although he was following the precepts of Zola in his novels of the '80s, their tone and attitude are closer to the fiction of Alphonse Daudet. The lack of critical and financial success for his novels during this period led him to try writing for the theatre. (His dramatic works and his experiences with theatre are discussed below.)

In the last quarter of 1889, he started translating "for pure and copious lucre" Port Tarascon, the third volume of Alphonse Daudet adventures of Tartarin de Tarascon. Serialized in Harper's Monthly Magazine from June 1890, this translation praised as "clever" by The Spectator was published in January 1891 by Sampson Low, Marston, Searle & Rivington.

After the stage failure of Guy Domville in 1895, James was near despair and thoughts of death plagued him. The years spent on dramatic works were not entirely a loss. As he moved into the last phase of his career he found ways to adapt dramatic techniques into the novel form.

In the late 1880s and throughout the 1890s James made several trips through Europe. He spent a long stay in Italy in 1887. In that year the short novel The Aspern Papers and The Reverberator were published.

Late years, 1898–1916

In 1897–1898 he moved to Rye, Sussex, and wrote The Turn of the Screw. 1899–1900 saw the publication of The Awkward Age and The Sacred

Fount. During 1902–1904 he wrote The Ambassadors, The Wings of the Dove, and The Golden Bowl.

In 1904 he revisited America and lectured on Balzac. In 1906–1910 he published The American Scene and edited the "New York Edition", a 24-volume collection of his works. In 1910 his brother William died; Henry had just joined William from an unsuccessful search for relief in Europe on what then turned out to be his (Henry's) last visit to the United States (from summer 1910 to July 1911), and was near him, according to a letter he wrote, when he died.

In 1913 he wrote his autobiographies, A Small Boy and Others, and Notes of a Son and Brother. After the outbreak of the First World War in 1914 he did war work. In 1915 he became a British subject and was awarded the Order of Merit the following year. He died on 28 February 1916, in Chelsea, London. As he requested, his ashes were buried in Cambridge Cemetery in Massachusetts.

Biographers

James regularly rejected suggestions that he should marry, and after settling in London proclaimed himself "a bachelor". F. W. Dupee, in several volumes on the James family, originated the theory that he had been in love with his cousin Mary ("Minnie") Temple, but that a neurotic fear of sex kept him from admitting such affections: "James's invalidism ... was itself the symptom of some fear of or scruple against sexual love on his part." Dupee used an episode from James's memoir A Small Boy and Others, recounting a dream of a Napoleonic image in the Louvre, to exemplify James's romanticism about Europe, a Napoleonic fantasy into which he fled.

Dupee had not had access to the James family papers and worked principally from James's published memoir of his older brother, William, and the limited collection of letters edited by Percy Lubbock, heavily weighted toward James's last years. His account therefore moved directly from James's childhood, when he trailed after his older brother, to elderly invalidism. As more material became available to scholars, including the diaries of contemporaries and hundreds of affectionate and sometimes erotic letters written by James to younger men, the picture of neurotic celibacy gave way to a portrait of a closeted homosexual.

Between 1953 and 1972, Leon Edel authored a major five-volume biography of James, which accessed unpublished letters and documents after Edel gained the permission of James's family. Edel's portrayal of James included the suggestion he was celibate. It was a view first propounded by critic Saul Rosenzweig in 1943. In 1996 Sheldon M. Novick published Henry James: The Young Master, followed by Henry James: The Mature Master (2007). The first book "caused something of an uproar in Jamesian circles" as it challenged the previous received notion of celibacy, a once-familiar paradigm in biographies of homosexuals when direct evidence was non-existent. Novick also criticised Edel for following the discounted Freudian interpretation of homosexuality "as a kind of failure." The difference of opinion erupted in a series of exchanges between Edel and Novick which were published by the online magazine Slate, with the latter arguing that even the suggestion of celibacy went against James's own injunction "live!"—not "fantasize!"

A letter James wrote in old age to Hugh Walpole has been cited as an explicit statement of this. Walpole confessed to him of indulging in "high jinks", and James wrote a reply endorsing it: "We must know, as much as possible, in our beautiful art, yours & mine, what we are talking about — & the only way to know it is to have lived & loved & cursed & floundered & enjoyed & suffered — I don't think I regret a single 'excess' of my responsive youth".

The interpretation of James as living a less austere emotional life has been subsequently explored by other scholars. The often intense politics of Jamesian scholarship has also been the subject of studies. Author Colm Tóibín has said that Eve Kosofsky Sedgwick's Epistemology of the Closet made a landmark difference to Jamesian scholarship by arguing that he be read as a homosexual writer whose desire to keep his sexuality a secret shaped his layered style and dramatic artistry. According to Tóibín such a reading "removed James from the realm of dead white males who wrote about posh people. He became our contemporary."

James's letters to expatriate American sculptor Hendrik Christian Andersen have attracted particular attention. James met the 27-year-old Andersen in Rome in 1899, when James was 56, and wrote letters to Andersen that are intensely emotional: "I hold you, dearest boy, in my innermost love, & count on your feeling me—in every throb of your soul". In a letter of 6 May 1904, to his brother William, James referred to himself as "always your hopelessly celibate even though sexagenarian Henry". How accurate that description might have been is the subject of contention among James's biographers, but the letters to Andersen were occasionally quasi-erotic: "I put, my dear boy, my arm around you, & feel the pulsation, thereby, as it were, of our excellent future & your admirable endowment." To his homosexual friend Howard Sturgis, James could write: "I repeat, almost to indiscretion, that I could live with you. Meanwhile I can only try to live without you."

His numerous letters to the many young gay men among his close male friends are more forthcoming. In a letter to Howard Sturgis, following a long visit, James refers jocularly to their "happy little congress of two" and in letters to Hugh Walpole he pursues convoluted jokes and puns about their relationship, referring to himself as an elephant who "paws you oh so benevolently" and winds about Walpole his "well meaning old trunk". His letters to Walter Berry printed by the Black Sun Press have long been celebrated for their lightly veiled eroticism.

He corresponded in almost equally extravagant language with his many female friends, writing, for example, to fellow novelist Lucy Clifford: "Dearest Lucy! What shall I say? when I love you so very, very much, and see you nine times for once that I see Others! Therefore I think that—if you want it made clear to the meanest intelligence—I love you more than I love Others." To his New York friend Mary Cadwalader Jones: "Dearest Mary Cadwalader. I yearn over you, but I yearn in vain; & your long silence really breaks my heart, mystifies, depresses, almost alarms me, to the point even of making me wonder if poor unconscious & doting old Célimare [Jones's pet name for James] has 'done' anything, in some dark somnambulism of the spirit, which has ... given you a bad moment, or a wrong impression, or a 'colourable pretext' ... However these things may be, he loves you as tenderly as ever;

nothing, to the end of time, will ever detach him from you, & he remembers those Eleventh St. matutinal intimes hours, those telephonic matinées, as the most romantic of his life ..." His long friendship with American novelist Constance Fenimore Woolson, in whose house he lived for a number of weeks in Italy in 1887, and his shock and grief over her suicide in 1894, are discussed in detail in Edel's biography and play a central role in a study by Lyndall Gordon. (Edel conjectured that Woolson was in love with James and killed herself in part because of his coldness, but Woolson's biographers have objected to Edel's account.)

Works

Style and themes

James is one of the major figures of trans-Atlantic literature. His works frequently juxtapose characters from the Old World (Europe), embodying a feudal civilisation that is beautiful, often corrupt, and alluring, and from the New World (United States), where people are often brash, open, and assertive and embody the virtues—freedom and a more highly evolved moral character—of the new American society. James explores this clash of personalities and cultures, in stories of personal relationships in which power is exercised well or badly. His protagonists were often young American women facing oppression or abuse, and as his secretary Theodora Bosanquet remarked in her monograph Henry James at Work:

> When he walked out of the refuge of his study and into the world and looked around him, he saw a place of torment, where creatures of prey perpetually thrust their claws into the quivering flesh of doomed, defenseless children of light ... His novels are a repeated exposure of this wickedness, a reiterated and passionate plea for the fullest freedom of development, unimperiled by reckless and barbarous stupidity.

Critics have jokingly described three phases in the development of James's prose: "James I, James II, and The Old Pretender." He wrote short stories and plays. Finally, in his third and last period he returned to the long, serialised novel. Beginning in the second period, but most noticeably in the third, he increasingly abandoned direct statement in favour of frequent double negatives, and complex descriptive imagery. Single paragraphs began to run for page after page, in which an initial noun would be succeeded by pronouns surrounded by clouds of adjectives and prepositional clauses, far from their original referents, and verbs would be deferred and then preceded by a series of adverbs. The overall effect could be a vivid evocation of a scene as perceived by a sensitive observer. It has been debated whether this change of style was engendered by James's shifting from writing to dictating to a typist, a change made during the composition of What Maisie Knew.

In its intense focus on the consciousness of his major characters, James's later work foreshadows extensive developments in 20th century fiction. Indeed, he might have influenced stream-of-consciousness writers such as Virginia Woolf, who not only read some of his novels but also wrote essays about them. Both contemporary and modern readers have found the late style difficult and unnecessary; his friend Edith Wharton, who admired him greatly, said that there were passages in his work that were all but incomprehensible. James was harshly portrayed by H. G. Wells as a hippopotamus laboriously attempting to pick up a pea that had got into a corner of its cage. The "late James" style was ably parodied by Max Beerbohm in "The Mote in the Middle Distance".

More important for his work overall may have been his position as an expatriate, and in other ways an outsider, living in Europe. While he came from middle-class and provincial beginnings (seen from the perspective of European polite society) he worked very hard to gain access to all levels of society, and the settings of his fiction range from working class to aristocratic, and often describe the efforts of middle-class Americans to make their way in European capitals. He confessed he got some of his best story ideas from gossip at the dinner table or at country house weekends. He worked for a living, however, and lacked the experiences of select schools, university, and army service, the common bonds of masculine society. He was furthermore a man whose tastes and interests were, according to the prevailing standards of Victorian era Anglo-American culture, rather feminine, and who was shadowed by the cloud of prejudice that then and later accompanied suspicions of his homosexuality. Edmund Wilson famously compared James's objectivity to Shakespeare's:

One would be in a position to appreciate James better if one compared him with the dramatists of the seventeenth century—Racine and Molière, whom he resembles in form as well as in point of view, and even Shakespeare, when allowances are made for the most extreme differences in subject and form. These poets are not, like Dickens and Hardy, writers of melodrama—either humorous or pessimistic, nor secretaries of society like Balzac, nor prophets like Tolstoy: they are occupied simply with the presentation of conflicts of moral character, which they do not concern themselves about softening or averting. They do not indict society for these situations: they regard them as universal and inevitable. They do not even blame God for allowing them: they accept them as the conditions of life.

It is also possible to see many of James's stories as psychological thought-experiments. In his preface to the New York edition of The American he describes the development of the story in his mind as exactly such: the "situation" of an American, "some robust but insidiously beguiled and betrayed, some cruelly wronged, compatriot..." with the focus of the story being on the response of this wronged man. The Portrait of a Lady may be an experiment to see what happens when an idealistic young woman suddenly becomes very rich. In many of his tales, characters seem to exemplify alternative futures and possibilities, as most markedly in "The Jolly Corner", in which the protagonist and a ghost-doppelganger live alternative American and European lives; and in others, like The Ambassadors, an older James seems fondly to regard his own younger self facing a crucial moment.

Major novels

The first period of James's fiction, usually considered to have culminated in The Portrait of a Lady, concentrated on the contrast between Europe and America. The style of these novels is generally straightforward and, though personally characteristic, well within the norms of 19th-century fiction. Roderick Hudson (1875) is a Künstlerroman that traces the development of the title character, an extremely talented sculptor. Although the book shows some signs of immaturity—this was James's first serious attempt at a full-length novel—it has attracted favourable comment due to the vivid realisation of the three major characters: Roderick Hudson, superbly gifted but unstable and unreliable; Rowland Mallet, Roderick's limited but much more mature friend and patron; and Christina Light, one of James's most enchanting and maddening femmes fatales. The pair of Hudson and Mallet has been seen as representing the two sides of James's own nature: the wildly imaginative artist and the brooding conscientious mentor.

In The Portrait of a Lady (1881) James concluded the first phase of his career with a novel that remains his most popular piece of long fiction. The story is of a spirited young American woman, Isabel Archer, who "affronts her destiny" and finds it overwhelming. She inherits a large amount of money and subsequently becomes the victim of Machiavellian scheming by two American expatriates. The narrative is set mainly in Europe, especially in England and Italy. Generally regarded as the masterpiece of his early phase, The Portrait of a Lady is described as a psychological novel, exploring the minds of his characters, and almost a work of social science, exploring the differences between Europeans and Americans, the old and the new worlds.

The second period of James's career, which extends from the publication of The Portrait of a Lady through the end of the nineteenth century, features less popular novels including The Princess Casamassima, published serially in The Atlantic Monthly in 1885–1886, and The Bostonians, published serially in The Century Magazine during the same period. This period also featured James's celebrated Gothic novella, The Turn of the Screw.

The third period of James's career reached its most significant achievement in three novels published just around the start of the 20th century: The Wings of the Dove (1902), The Ambassadors (1903), and The Golden Bowl (1904). Critic F. O. Matthiessen called this "trilogy" James's major phase, and these novels have certainly received intense critical study. It was the second-written of the books, The Wings of the Dove (1902) that was the first published because it attracted no serialization. This novel tells the story of Milly Theale, an American heiress stricken with a serious disease, and her impact on the people around her. Some of these people befriend Milly with honourable motives, while others are more self-interested. James stated in his autobiographical books that Milly was based on Minny Temple, his beloved cousin who died at an early age of tuberculosis. He said that he attempted in the novel to wrap her memory in the "beauty and dignity of art".

Shorter narratives

James was particularly interested in what he called the "beautiful and blest nouvelle", or the longer form of short narrative. Still, he produced a number of very short stories in which he achieved notable compression of sometimes complex subjects. The following narratives are representative of James's achievement in the shorter forms of fiction.

- "A Tragedy of Error" (1864), short story

- "The Story of a Year" (1865), short story

- A Passionate Pilgrim (1871), novella

- Madame de Mauves (1874), novella

- Daisy Miller (1878), novella

- The Aspern Papers (1888), novella

- The Lesson of the Master (1888), novella

- The Pupil (1891), short story

- "The Figure in the Carpet" (1896), short story

- The Beast in the Jungle (1903), novella

- An International Episode (1878)

- Picture and Text

- Four Meetings (1885)

- A London Life, and Other Tales (1889)

- The Spoils of Poynton (1896)

- Embarrassments (1896)

- The Two Magics: The Turn of the Screw, Covering End (1898)

- A Little Tour of France (1900)

- The Sacred Fount (1901)

- Views and Reviews (1908)

- The Wings of the Dove, Volume I (1902)

- The Wings of the Dove, Volume II (1909)

- The Finer Grain (1910)

- The Outcry (1911)

- Lady Barbarina: The Siege of London, An International Episode and Other Tales (1922)

- The Birthplace (1922)

Plays

At several points in his career James wrote plays, beginning with one-act plays written for periodicals in 1869 and 1871 and a dramatisation of his popular novella Daisy Miller in 1882. From 1890 to 1892, having received a bequest that freed him from magazine publication, he made a strenuous effort to succeed on the London stage, writing a half-dozen plays of which only one, a dramatisation of his novel The American, was produced. This play was performed for several years by a touring repertory company and had a respectable run in London, but did not earn very much money for James. His other plays written at this time were not produced.

In 1893, however, he responded to a request from actor-manager George Alexander for a serious play for the opening of his renovated St. James's Theatre, and wrote a long drama, Guy Domville, which Alexander produced. There was a noisy uproar on the opening night, 5 January 1895, with hissing from the gallery when James took his bow after the final curtain, and the author was upset. The play received moderately good reviews and had a modest run of four weeks before being taken off to make way for Oscar Wilde's The Importance of Being Earnest, which Alexander thought would have better prospects for the coming season.

After the stresses and disappointment of these efforts James insisted that he would write no more for the theatre, but within weeks had agreed to write a curtain-raiser for Ellen Terry. This became the one-act "Summersoft", which he later rewrote into a short story, "Covering End", and then expanded into a full-length play, The High Bid, which had a brief run in London in 1907, when James made another concerted effort to write for the stage. He wrote three new plays, two of which were in production when the death of Edward VII on 6 May 1910 plunged London into mourning and theatres closed. Discouraged by failing health and the stresses of theatrical work, James did not renew his efforts in the theatre, but recycled his plays as successful novels. The Outcry was a best-seller in the United States when it was published in 1911. During the years 1890–1893 when he was most engaged with the theatre, James wrote a good deal of theatrical criticism and assisted Elizabeth Robins and others in translating and producing Henrik Ibsen for the first time in London.

Leon Edel argued in his psychoanalytic biography that James was traumatised by the opening night uproar that greeted Guy Domville, and that it plunged him into a prolonged depression. The successful later novels, in Edel's view, were the result of a kind of self-analysis, expressed in fiction, which partly freed him from his fears. Other biographers and scholars have not accepted this account, however; the more common view being that of F.O. Matthiessen, who wrote: "Instead of being crushed by the collapse of his hopes [for the theatre]... he felt a resurgence of new energy."

Non-fiction

Beyond his fiction, James was one of the more important literary critics in the history of the novel. In his classic essay The Art of Fiction (1884), he argued against rigid prescriptions on the novelist's choice of subject and method of treatment. He maintained that the widest possible freedom in content and approach would help ensure narrative fiction's continued vitality.

135

James wrote many valuable critical articles on other novelists; typical is his book-length study of Nathaniel Hawthorne, which has been the subject of critical debate. Richard Brodhead has suggested that the study was emblematic of James's struggle with Hawthorne's influence, and constituted an effort to place the elder writer "at a disadvantage." Gordon Fraser, meanwhile, has suggested that the study was part of a more commercial effort by James to introduce himself to British readers as Hawthorne's natural successor.

When James assembled the New York Edition of his fiction in his final years, he wrote a series of prefaces that subjected his own work to searching, occasionally harsh criticism.

At 22 James wrote The Noble School of Fiction for The Nation's first issue in 1865. He would write, in all, over 200 essays and book, art, and theatre reviews for the magazine.

For most of his life James harboured ambitions for success as a playwright. He converted his novel The American into a play that enjoyed modest returns in the early 1890s. In all he wrote about a dozen plays, most of which went unproduced. His costume drama Guy Domville failed disastrously on its opening night in 1895. James then largely abandoned his efforts to conquer the stage and returned to his fiction. In his Notebooks he maintained that his theatrical experiment benefited his novels and tales by helping him dramatise his characters' thoughts and emotions. James produced a small but valuable amount of theatrical criticism, including perceptive appreciations of Henrik Ibsen.

With his wide-ranging artistic interests, James occasionally wrote on the visual arts. Perhaps his most valuable contribution was his favourable assessment of fellow expatriate John Singer Sargent, a painter whose critical status has improved markedly in recent decades. James also wrote sometimes charming, sometimes brooding articles about various places he visited and lived in. His most famous books of travel writing include Italian Hours (an example of the charming approach) and The American Scene (most definitely on the brooding side).

James was one of the great letter-writers of any era. More than ten thousand of his personal letters are extant, and over three thousand have been published in a large number of collections. A complete edition of James's letters began publication in 2006, edited by Pierre Walker and Greg Zacharias. As of 2014, eight volumes have been published, covering the period from 1855 to 1880. James's correspondents included celebrated contemporaries like Robert Louis Stevenson, Edith Wharton and Joseph Conrad, along with many others in his wide circle of friends and acquaintances. The letters range from the "mere twaddle of graciousness" to serious discussions of artistic, social and personal issues.

Very late in life James began a series of autobiographical works: A Small Boy and Others, Notes of a Son and Brother, and the unfinished The Middle Years. These books portray the development of a classic observer who was passionately interested in artistic creation but was somewhat reticent about participating fully in the life around him.

Reception

Criticism, biographies and fictional treatments

James's work has remained steadily popular with the limited audience of educated readers to whom he spoke during his lifetime, and has remained firmly in the canon, but, after his death, some American critics, such as Van Wyck Brooks, expressed hostility towards James for his long expatriation and eventual naturalisation as a British subject. Other critics such as E. M. Forster complained about what they saw as James's squeamishness in the treatment of sex and other possibly controversial material, or dismissed his late style as difficult and obscure, relying heavily on extremely long sentences and excessively latinate language. Similarly Oscar Wilde criticised him for writing "fiction as if it were a painful duty". Vernon Parrington, composing a canon of American literature, condemned James for having cut himself off from America. Jorge Luis Borges wrote about him, "Despite the scruples and delicate complexities of James, his work suffers from a major defect: the absence of life." And Virginia Woolf, writing to Lytton Strachey, asked, "Please tell me what you find in Henry James. ... we have his works here, and

I read, and I can't find anything but faintly tinged rose water, urbane and sleek, but vulgar and pale as Walter Lamb. Is there really any sense in it?" The novelist W. Somerset Maugham wrote, "He did not know the English as an Englishman instinctively knows them and so his English characters never to my mind quite ring true," and argued "The great novelists, even in seclusion, have lived life passionately. Henry James was content to observe it from a window." Maugham nevertheless wrote, "The fact remains that those last novels of his, notwithstanding their unreality, make all other novels, except the very best, unreadable." Colm Tóibín observed that James "never really wrote about the English very well. His English characters don't work for me."

Despite these criticisms, James is now valued for his psychological and moral realism, his masterful creation of character, his low-key but playful humour, and his assured command of the language. In his 1983 book, The Novels of Henry James, Edward Wagenknecht offers an assessment that echoes Theodora Bosanquet's:

> "To be completely great," Henry James wrote in an early review, "a work of art must lift up the heart," and his own novels do this to an outstanding degree ... More than sixty years after his death, the great novelist who sometimes professed to have no opinions stands foursquare in the great Christian humanistic and democratic tradition. The men and women who, at the height of World War II, raided the secondhand shops for his out-of-print books knew what they were about. For no writer ever raised a braver banner to which all who love freedom might adhere.

William Dean Howells saw James as a representative of a new realist school of literary art which broke with the English romantic tradition epitomised by the works of Charles Dickens and William Makepeace Thackeray. Howells wrote that realism found "its chief exemplar in Mr. James... A novelist he is not, after the old fashion, or after any fashion but his own." F.R. Leavis championed Henry James as a novelist of "established pre-eminence" in The Great Tradition (1948), asserting that The Portrait of a Lady and The Bostonians were "the two most brilliant novels in the language." James is now prized as a master of point of view who moved literary fiction forward by insisting in showing, not telling, his stories to the reader. (Source: Wikipedia)

NOTABLE WORKS

NOVELS

Watch and Ward (1871)

Roderick Hudson (1875)

The American (1877)

The Europeans (1878)

Confidence (1879)

Washington Square (1880)

The Portrait of a Lady (1881)

The Bostonians (1886)

The Princess Casamassima (1886)

The Reverberator (1888)

The Tragic Muse (1890)

The Other House (1896)

The Spoils of Poynton (1897)

What Maisie Knew (1897)

The Awkward Age (1899)

The Sacred Fount (1901)

The Wings of the Dove (1902)

The Ambassadors (1903)

The Golden Bowl (1904)

The Whole Family (collaborative novel with eleven other authors, 1908)

The Outcry (1911)

The Ivory Tower (unfinished, published posthumously 1917)

The Sense of the Past (unfinished, published posthumously 1917)

SHORT STORIES AND NOVELLAS

A Tragedy of Error (1864)

The Story of a Year (1865)

A Landscape Painter (1866)

A Day of Days (1866)

My Friend Bingham (1867)

Poor Richard (1867)

The Story of a Masterpiece (1868)

A Most Extraordinary Case (1868)

A Problem (1868)

De Grey: A Romance (1868)

Osborne's Revenge (1868)

The Romance of Certain Old Clothes (1868)

A Light Man (1869)

Gabrielle de Bergerac (1869)

Travelling Companions (1870)

A Passionate Pilgrim (1871)

At Isella (1871)

Master Eustace (1871)

Guest's Confession (1872)

The Madonna of the Future (1873)

The Sweetheart of M. Briseux (1873)

The Last of the Valerii (1874)

Madame de Mauves (1874)

Adina (1874)

Professor Fargo (1874)

Eugene Pickering (1874)

Benvolio (1875)

Crawford's Consistency (1876)

The Ghostly Rental (1876)

Four Meetings (1877)

Rose-Agathe (1878, as Théodolinde)

Daisy Miller (1878)

Longstaff's Marriage (1878)

An International Episode (1878)

The Pension Beaurepas (1879)

A Diary of a Man of Fifty (1879)

A Bundle of Letters (1879)

The Point of View (1882)

The Siege of London (1883)

Impressions of a Cousin (1883)

Lady Barberina (1884)

Pandora (1884)

The Author of Beltraffio (1884)

Georgina's Reasons (1884)

A New England Winter (1884)

The Path of Duty (1884)

Mrs. Temperly (1887)

Louisa Pallant (1888)

The Aspern Papers (1888)

The Liar (1888)

The Modern Warning (1888, originally published as The Two Countries)

A London Life (1888)

The Patagonia (1888)

The Lesson of the Master (1888)

The Solution (1888)

The Pupil (1891)

Brooksmith (1891)

The Marriages (1891)

The Chaperon (1891)

Sir Edmund Orme (1891)

Nona Vincent (1892)

The Real Thing (1892)

The Private Life (1892)

Lord Beaupré (1892)

The Visits (1892)

Sir Dominick Ferrand (1892)

Greville Fane (1892)

Collaboration (1892)

Owen Wingrave (1892)

The Wheel of Time (1892)

The Middle Years (1893)

The Death of the Lion (1894)

The Coxon Fund (1894)

The Next Time (1895)

Glasses (1896)

The Altar of the Dead (1895)

The Figure in the Carpet (1896)

The Way It Came (1896, also published as The Friends of the Friends)

The Turn of the Screw (1898)

Covering End (1898)

In the Cage (1898)

John Delavoy (1898)

The Given Case (1898)

Europe (1899)

The Great Condition (1899)

The Real Right Thing (1899)

Paste (1899)

The Great Good Place (1900)

Maud-Evelyn (1900)

Miss Gunton of Poughkeepsie (1900)

The Tree of Knowledge (1900)

The Abasement of the Northmores (1900)

The Third Person (1900)

The Special Type (1900)

The Tone of Time (1900)

Broken Wings (1900)

The Two Faces (1900)

Mrs. Medwin (1901)

The Beldonald Holbein (1901)

The Story in It (1902)

Flickerbridge (1902)

The Birthplace (1903)

The Beast in the Jungle (1903)

The Papers (1903)

Fordham Castle (1904)

Julia Bride (1908)

The Jolly Corner (1908)

The Velvet Glove (1909)

Mora Montravers (1909)

Crapy Cornelia (1909)

The Bench of Desolation (1909)

A Round of Visits (1910)

OTHER

Transatlantic Sketches (1875)

French Poets and Novelists (1878)

Hawthorne (1879)

Portraits of Places (1883)

A Little Tour in France (1884)

Partial Portraits (1888)

Essays in London and Elsewhere (1893)

Picture and Text (1893)

Terminations (1893)

Theatricals (1894)

Theatricals: Second Series (1895)

Guy Domville (1895)

The Soft Side (1900)

William Wetmore Story and His Friends (1903)

The Better Sort (1903)

English Hours (1905)

The Question of our Speech; The Lesson of Balzac. Two Lectures (1905)

The American Scene (1907)

Views and Reviews (1908)

Italian Hours (1909)

A Small Boy and Others (1913)

Notes on Novelists (1914)

Notes of a Son and Brother (1914)

Within the Rim (1918)

Travelling Companions (1919)

Notebooks (various, published posthumously)

The Middle Years (unfinished, published posthumously 1917)

A Most Unholy Trade (1925, published posthumously)

The Art of the Novel : Critical Prefaces (1934)

CPSIA information can be obtained
at www.ICGtesting.com
Printed in the USA
LVHW040135031120
670492LV00021B/704